MW00775432

Misery Range

Bay of
Bountiful

Eden Glade

Mt
Molar

Twisty River

Grandad's
Gully

Cascade Canyon

Puzzling
Plains

Col

Cliffs
of
Calamity

Mt
Monstrous

Mother's
Knee Hill

Ridge of Rising
Flame

Swamp of
Children's Wishes

Tree of Wailing
Witches

Meadow of
Dreams

Ancient
Forest

Mystic

Lunch
Pass

Home

The
ISLAND

Home
Lagoon

Granny's Pass

Paradise Peninsula

Basin
Three Sisters
Bow Beach
N
W
S
Pancake Rocks
Forest
Fox Glacier
Fearsome Fjords
Mt Difficulty
Dragon's Crater
Putrid Plains
Clappers' Saddle
Eastern Bays
tains
Mt Astonishing
Gulp Swallow Pass
Magic Terraces
Boiling Stream
Fairy Falls
Lake Levitation
zor Reef

*For the Russell boys*
*– GKK, F, and P*
-JR

Published by Dragon Brothers Books Ltd
www.dragonbrothersbooks.com
© 2020 James Russell. Illustrations © 2020 Dragon Brothers Books.
A catalogue record for this book is available from the National Library of New Zealand. The
moral rights of the author have been asserted. This book is copyright. Except for the purposes
of fair reviewing no part of this publication may be reproduced or transmitted in any form or
by any means, electronic or mechanical, including photocopying or recording, or stored in any
information storage and retrieval system, without permission in writing from the publisher.
ISBN: 978-0-473-51725-0
Digital animations created by Courtney White
Cover illustration: Kerem Beyit
Internal vignettes: Suleyman Temiz
Editing: Anna Bowles
App development: Freddy Weng
Design: Suzanne Denmead
Chapter icon: istock

# THE DRAGON DEFENDERS

## BOOK FIVE

*The Grand Opening*

A Dragon Brothers Book by

# JAMES RUSSELL

*"So good you'll feel empty when you finish it."*

Odette Ala'alatoa-Dale, age 8

*"So gripping we couldn't put it down! You never knew what was going to happen next!"*

Liam and Harry Rippingale, age 12 and 9

*"Definitely the best in the series. I never wanted it to end!"*

Sadie Atkins, age 8

*"The best one yet!"*

Brennan Hosking, age 11

*"...took me into the deepest despair, then showed me what happens when you don't give up!"*

Jaeda Ala'alatoa-Dale, age 11

*"Action-packed from the moment you open the cover!"*

Madison Phillips, age 11

# www.dragonbrothersbooks.com

## Sign up to find out when the next chapter book in the series comes out.

Simply visit **www.dragonbrothersbooks.com** and enter your email address. We'll keep you updated on new books, and we'll send you an email whenever anything cool happens!

Books in the series

   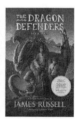 

*Or, for younger readers*

The Dragon Brothers Trilogy

The Dragon Defenders series grew out of The Dragon Brothers Trilogy
– children's picture books for children aged 3-7.

## How to use this book

This book is unlike any other you've seen. Of course, it works just like a normal book; you start reading at the start, and read right through to the end. That will work just fine.

But you can also enjoy it another way. You can download the free 'AR Reads' app onto a smartphone or tablet, point it at parts of the book and watch it become reality.

Your choice!

**Here's how:**

**Step 1.** Download the free 'AR Reads' app*.
You'll find this on the App Store, or on Google Play.

**Step 2.** Start up the app.

**Step 3.** Follow the set-up instructions.

**Step 4.** Point your device's camera at the pictures on the pages marked with a phone/tablet at the bottom.

*If you already have the AR Reads app downloaded onto your device, you'll need to check for updates in order for the app to work on The Dragon Defenders – Book Four.
To use this app, your device will need to have an internet connection.

# CHAPTER 1

P addy made a face at the boy in the mirror. He didn't like the look of him. In fact, he hardly recognised him. He was dressed in school uniform – a light blue shirt and grey shorts, with a navy tie fastened so tightly around his neck he felt as though he was being choked. What sort of an idiot invented the tie, Paddy wondered. Why would you ever voluntarily put yourself through the discomfort of having something wrapped tightly around your neck, while at the same time putting up with a pointless, flapping piece of cloth whipping about in the wind? It was bound to snag on something sooner or later.

When he'd arrived here, at his grandparents' home, he couldn't stop looking in the mirror – it was the first time he'd ever really seen himself, except for dark and wobbly reflections in rock pools. But now he could hardly stand the sight.

Paddy wanted to rip the tie from his neck, but he knew he wasn't allowed. Apparently all schoolchildren had to be dressed identically. Another stupid rule.

"Hurry up, Paddy! We can't be late for our first day of school!" His brother's voice echoed down the hall from the kitchen. Flynn sounded excited, as if he was actually looking forward to it.

Paddy ignored him. He ran his fingers through his hair, and then messed it up fiercely, making it stick out in all directions. 'That's better', he thought. But it was only a small act of defiance, and it failed to lift his spirits. Anger still seethed through him like electricity. He sat down on the edge of the bath.

"Paddy?"

He looked up. His mother stood in the doorway, her face the picture of concern.

"Are you ready?"

"No," he replied grumpily, then immediately he felt bad. This wasn't her fault.

"Come on," she said. "It'll be fun – you'll see. The principal was lovely and the teachers seem nice. You'll love it."

"I won't. I'll hate it," he said. "Why do we have to go?"

"Because it's illegal not to, for one thing. Your father and I will get into trouble if we don't send you to school."

"Can't we just go back to The Island?" he pleaded, but he already knew the answer. Just last night they'd felt a powerful tremor shaking the house while they were getting ready for bed. Another earthquake. If they could feel it here on the mainland, it must have been enormous on The Island, perhaps even large enough to set off another tsunami. It was the third earthquake they'd felt in the week since the violent eruptions of Mt Astonishing had driven them from the paradise where they had grown up.

"The mountain might erupt for some time yet," reasoned his mother. "It could be days or weeks, but it could also be months or years. We just don't know. We have to be patient. And, while we're here, you boys, and Briar, have to go to school. It's the law." She gave Paddy a hug. "Come on," she said. "Time to go."

Paddy stood up and walked slowly along the hallway, dragging his feet, which were encased in heavy, black school shoes. He felt constricted, suffocated – and not just by the uniform. Life seemed to be collapsing in on him from all sides. Their island was uninhabitable, their house completely destroyed. All of them – his grandparents, parents, Flynn, Briar, Ada and himself, were now shoehorned into his grandparents' three-bedroomed home. Outside there was no forest, no sea, no mountains anywhere near them – just endless concrete and thousands of fenced-off buildings in every direction. Coco their dog was confined to the backyard, no longer able to roam free. Clappers – their poor horse – was imprisoned too, trapped in a small paddock encircled by an electric fence, at a farm two miles away from the house. Although they'd saved her from The Island, Paddy couldn't help but think that she'd have been happier left there, taking her chances against the volcano. Even Lightning, the boys' falcon, who could fly where he pleased, seemed lost. He perched for hours on the windowsill, unmoving, barely picking at the scraps of meat they gave him.

But what really broke Paddy's heart was when he thought of their dragons – Elton, Iris, and their brand-new baby, Ahi. There had been no choice but to leave them on The Island at the mercy of the erupting volcano. He'd never forget the look of confusion and fear on Elton's face as he, Flynn and Briar had turned away from the dragons, leaving the island on his grandparents' yacht.

As if that wasn't awful enough, they'd been at sea for no more than an hour when a huge swarm of black helicopters appeared on the horizon, speeding towards The Island. Even before he'd seen the dogs' heads painted on their sides, Paddy knew that the helicopters belonged to The Pitbull, the evil boss from the mainland and Briar's uncle, who was hell-bent on capturing the dragons to make himself rich and famous. He and Flynn and, he had to admit, Briar, had thwarted The Pitbull so far, but now it seemed that nothing could stand in his way.

The final blow had come when Paddy saw the look on Briar's face. She'd looked haunted, guilty –

so guilty that she couldn't hide it from the brothers. The pieces of the puzzle had snapped rapidly into place in Paddy's mind. The brothers had entrusted Briar with the phone they had stolen from The Pitbull's men, and she had betrayed them, using it to call The Pitbull. She had told him exactly where the dragons were, and to come and capture them when they were at their most vulnerable.

He hadn't spoken to Briar since – not one word.

Now it was driving him mad that he had no idea if the dragons had been captured, or whether they had somehow evaded the helicopters and were still on The Island. Even if they'd escaped, they might all be dead by now, killed by falling rocks. Either possibility was too horrifying to consider.

Paddy walked into the kitchen. Flynn was trying to feed Lightning, who was perched on his shoulder.

"Hey," he said, smiling. "Come on, let's go."

Paddy ignored him. Briar stood in the doorway and Paddy pushed past her and stepped out into the cool morning. For an instant, he expected to see trees, birds, sea and sparkling white sand. But, instead, he was met with fences, gates, concrete, and cars, and his mood blackened further.

Paddy set off towards the school. He walked well ahead of Briar and his brother, but he could still hear them chatting and ground his teeth in resentment. He couldn't believe his brother was taking her side; he'd never felt so betrayed. Flynn kept calling out to him to walk with them, but Paddy didn't reply and Flynn eventually gave up.

The walk to their new school was a little under two miles – or three kilometres, as they said here on the mainland – and halfway along they passed a row of shops selling a bewildering array of pointless things. At one end was a larger building – his grandmother called it a 'supermarket'. Paddy had visited it with her, and his eyes had nearly fallen out of his head when he saw all the vegetables lined up right along the length of one huge wall. But that turned out to be only the beginning. It continued for row upon row, more food than his family could eat in a lifetime. He couldn't figure out what half of it was, or why it all had to be packaged into boxes, bags and tins. Much of the food didn't look like food at all, made of strange substances and formed into unappetising shapes.

Paddy was passing the same supermarket now, and he happened to look up. Mounted on its roof was a giant board, thirty feet long and twenty high. His grandmother had told him it was called an advertising billboard. Yesterday it had displayed a picture of something called a 'Mega Burger'. But today a new advertisement had taken its place, one that made Paddy's heart stop and his knees give way. He grabbed and pulled at his tie as he struggled to breathe. Paddy heard Flynn and Briar's footsteps behind him as they rushed to help, but their gasps told him that they had seen it too.

Splashed across a lurid backdrop of fake flames and smoke was a picture of their wonderful dragon, Elton. His wings were outstretched, his talons curled as though he was bearing down upon the people walking along the footpath. His mouth was twisted into an ugly, ferocious snarl. Paddy had never seen him look like that in his life. Emblazoned across the bottom of the billboard were words more awful than Paddy could ever have imagined: *Welcome to Dragon World! Grand Opening this Saturday night. Tickets available now!*

# CHAPTER 2

"**T**HAT'S ENOUGH!"

The Pitbull batted away the makeup artist's hand so violently that the brush she was holding clattered onto the floor.

"Let's get on with it!" he roared. "You idiots are wasting my time!"

The director, standing nearby, stammered an apology, and shooed away the makeup team. There were no less than six of them, for pity's sake!

This director had come highly recommended, but all The Pitbull saw was a pathetic, snivelling excuse for a man. The fool wore a yellow silk scarf around his neck and a pink beret on his head, and called everybody 'darling'. Someone had mentioned his name, but The Pitbull had made absolutely no effort to remember it.

"Ahem," coughed the director nervously. "The film crew is ready when you are, sir." The Pitbull was pleased to see the man's face had paled, and his hands were shaking.

The Pitbull clawed off the paper cape the makeup people had tied around his neck and flung it to the floor. He stalked out of the room and down the short corridor that led to the arena. Before he stepped out into it, he paused. He took a deep breath. The feeling of triumph returned, a warm glow that spread throughout his body and ended up as a broad smile upon his face. He'd done it! He'd captured every dragon on that accursed island – every last one! Sure, there had been some problems – one helicopter had been hit by flying rocks from the volcano and another had gone down in the sea –

but none of that mattered now. He'd assumed that the pilots of those helicopters were rescued, but he didn't much care. You can't make an omelette without breaking some eggs, he reasoned. And he, The Pitbull, was about to make history. He was about to launch the greatest show anyone had ever seen.

"Dragon World."

He whispered it under his breath. The words had a thrilling sound, a truly magical, mystical feel. The stadium outside was completely empty, save for the film crew and a few of his men, but standing here, he could almost hear the crowd chanting his name: "PIT-BULL! PIT-BULL!" No doubt his adoring public would christen him with another name in time – The Dragon Lord, or Master of Dragons, perhaps. On second thoughts, maybe he should give himself a name, in case they came up with something he didn't like.

Within half an hour of the tickets going on sale that morning, the first fourteen shows of Dragon World had sold out. Over two million tickets. The billboards had only been erected in the early hours!

The internet caught fire, and stories appeared on every news channel on the planet. The Dragon World website crashed from all the traffic, and was down for half an hour before they could get it working again. When it went back online, another twelve nights were sold almost instantly before it crashed again. People from all over the world were buying tickets. The Pitbull had set the price astronomically high, but now he wished he'd set it even higher. He'd already heard of people selling their possessions to buy tickets, and queuing outside banks waiting for them to open so that they could beg for loans. Some people were buying fifty tickets at a time – probably to re-sell again at a higher price, but he didn't care about that.

After less than four hours, his bank account contained more money than had passed through it in his entire life; he had to put his finger on the computer screen so he could be sure he was counting the right amount of zeros. All of his worries, his debts, the colossal bill for the purchase of the fleet of helicopters – wiped out, in a single morning!

He'd already decided to keep the choppers, and the pilots could join his permanent staff. He'd have them give a spectacular aerial display above the stadium on the opening night of Dragon World. Perhaps he could even re-create the capture of the dragons as part of the show.

One thing was certain; he didn't need to be paying this idiot of a director to be making a TV advertisement for Dragon World! But, then again, he didn't want to deprive the public of a chance to see him on their screens, in their homes. He was the hero of the hour, after all. In fact, he was the hero of the day, the week, the month, and the year. He was, without a doubt, the hero of his generation, perhaps even the greatest man to ever live on earth! People would want to see him, to praise him, to meet him. Of course, he had no interest in meeting any of them, but via their television screens it was easy.

Pushing open the door to the arena, The Pitbull stepped out into the vast space. It was empty and lifeless, but he could imagine it filled with swirling and swooping dragons, breathing fire and roaring furiously, while he, their master, ran the show from his raised bulletproof glass bulb, high above the crowd, at the centre of the universe.

# CHAPTER 3

After seeing the billboard, the rest of Briar's walk to school was a blur. She was only dimly aware of Flynn trudging beside her, his head bowed, but she was too shocked, too saddened, to talk to him. Her confidence in what she had done was badly shaken. Perhaps the dragons might have been better off staying on The Island? Some would have been killed, certainly, but maybe not all of them? For all she knew – for all any of them knew – as a species they may have been through a volcanic eruption before and survived, back before

the brothers' grandparents had ever set foot on
The Island.

She realised that none of that mattered now, that
what was done was done. She might have made
the wrong decision, but her intentions had been
good. But Paddy might never forgive her. He refused
to listen whenever Flynn tried to reason with him,
covering his ears or simply walking off. They'd even
fought a few times, wrestling with each other until
one of their parents broke them up. Flynn was clearly
upset too; he'd told her that he couldn't see a way of
healing the rift. He was at a loss as to how to get his
brother back, yet she knew that he didn't want to hurt
her either. He was obviously torn, pulled between his
loyalty to Paddy, but also believing in her. She felt a
terrible burden of guilt.

Lost in her thoughts, Briar had barely registered
entering the school grounds. But suddenly she
became aware that she, Flynn, and Paddy were
being stared at from all sides. The noisy hum of the
schoolyard had died away. Briar looked around

at the children, and realised they were staring at her, more than they were at Paddy and Flynn. Why? Was there something wrong with her uniform? She looked down, giving herself the once-over, and everything seemed fine. But now she could see children pointing at her, and whispering excitedly to each other.

"What the devil do you think you're playing at, young lady!?"

The voice thundered across the schoolyard, booming and angry. Briar looked up, and was shocked to see that one of the teachers, a tall, thin man with hunched shoulders and a rat-like face, was striding across the playground towards her. In his right hand he gripped a cane, which he swung to and fro as he walked. Briar stopped in her tracks. Ahead, she saw Paddy turn around and take a couple of steps back towards her protectively, forgetting himself for a moment.

"Who do you think you are?" the man bellowed, now just ten paces away from Briar, and pointing at her accusingly. "That is strictly forbidden! We have rules here!"

Briar's mind clouded over with panic. She couldn't think what she'd done to upset this man, who was almost upon her. To her horror, he raised the cane above his head, looking for all the world like he was going to strike her with it!

Suddenly, Briar realised what was causing such a stir. Lightning! The falcon was on her shoulder, sound asleep. He'd followed the children when they left the house and fluttered down to perch there, coming along for the ride. She'd thought nothing of it, being quite used to it by now. How stupid! She hadn't wanted to draw any unnecessary attention to herself or the brothers, and look what she'd done!

Briar didn't wait to see what the teacher intended to do. She grabbed Lightning and flung him into the air, commanding him home with a short, sharp whistle. The falcon flapped his wings groggily, shocked out of his sleep. Then, suddenly, Briar felt the teacher's bony fingers grip her shoulder.

At the same time, she heard a whistle as the cane cut through the air, narrowly missing Lightning.

"Hey! Don't do that!" yelled Briar.

"Shoo!" yelled the teacher, tightening his grip on the wriggling girl. "Shoo, you filthy bird!"

As Lightning rose up out of reach, the man stopped trying to hit him with his cane. He pulled Briar around to stand in front of him.

"Pets aren't allowed in this school – under any circumstances!" he hissed into Briar's face, his breath sour, his eyes narrow.

"Take your hands off her."

Flynn's voice was low, and full of menace. "Leave her alone. And don't you ever try to hurt that bird again."

The teacher's mouth dropped open in amazement. He released Briar and spun around. Flynn stood firm, the look in his eyes determined, his hands balled into fists. Briar could see he was shaking with anger.

Paddy appeared behind Flynn, a grim expression on his face. He, too, looked like he was about to fly at the teacher.

Briar was sure the teacher was going to explode. He was clearly enraged at being spoken to so rudely, but also unnerved by the obvious anger of the three children. Instead, however, he turned on his heel and stalked back towards the staff room. When he was a safe distance away, he turned.

"You three – to the principal's office. Now!"

# CHAPTER 4

**"I**s it real?"

"Is it... dead?"

The film crew stood around, looking
doubtfully at the huge dragon slumped on the floor.
It was as still as a stone, its bright green scales and
orange-tinged wings shimmering under the harsh
glare of the studio lights. Like the ridge of a mountain
range, the curve of its powerful neck broadened
across its back and narrowed again to its long,
graceful tail.

"It's obviously not real, but it's certainly realistic," said another one of the crew, a stick-thin young man with spiky hair and tattoos covering every inch of his forearms. "Who made it? That's amazing model work."

"SHUT UP!" barked The Pitbull. "It's alive, you fools. It's a real dragon!" In truth, though, The Pitbull wasn't sure if the creature was alive. He wondered if his men had given it too much tranquilliser and had actually killed it. It really wasn't moving – he couldn't even see it breathing. He cautiously stretched out his foot and kicked one of its talons, quickly retreating afterwards in case the creature stirred. It didn't respond.

'The show must go on,' he thought. He stood beside the great dragon's head. Its lip had pulled back slightly, and a glistening, curved fang could be seen. With great care The Pitbull placed one foot upon the creature's head. He turned to face the camera, and puffed out his chest. He fancied he looked like a big-game hunter who'd just brought down a man-eating lion or a wild elephant.

"Start filming," he ordered. "But focus the camera only on my face. When I snap my fingers, zoom back out so that you get the dragon in the frame."

"Er, with respect, sir…" began the director.

"Silence!" barked The Pitbull. "Do what you're told!"

The director nodded vigorously, backing away.

The Pitbull levelled a steely gaze at the camera lens. He took a deep breath.

"Soon, everything you thought you knew about the animal kingdom will be proved wrong," he began, his voice booming. "Myth will become legend and fantasy become fact!"

His voice rose as he said this, but now he lowered it again, and leaned forward slightly, smiling at the camera.

He used his best voice – his brave explorer voice – as he told the story of how he'd captured the dragons – single handedly. He embellished a little bit here, made up a little bit there, reasoning that the stupid public wouldn't know the difference.

Snapping his fingers furiously off camera, he saw the crew adjust the lens in response. He finished the advertisement with a flourish:

"I give you… Dragon World!"

His audience would now see him, The Master of Dragons, in his pose of complete dominance, his foot resting upon the head of the mighty beast he had conquered!

The Pitbull smiled generously at the camera and nodded, as though listening to his audience's warm praise. "You're welcome," he said.

The director stepped forward.

"And… cut!" he ordered. "Wonderful, sir. It will make a fine advertisement. A real sense of drama and suspense. You're a natural, sir."

"Shut up!" snapped The Pitbull. "Finish it by saying that tickets are available from the Dragon World website. Have it back to me by this afternoon. Now get out of my sight!"

# CHAPTER 5

Flynn, Paddy, and Briar left the principal's office and walked out into an empty schoolyard.

The bell had gone a long time ago, and all the children were in their classrooms.

"Wonderful. Now we get to make a grand entrance," said Briar sarcastically. She was obviously dreading the moment when all heads would turn to watch them walk in.

"It'll be fine," said Flynn. "Don't worry about it. It might be fun."

He was trying to sound optimistic, but inside Flynn was in turmoil. Going to the principal's office at the start of his first day of school had definitely not been part of his plan. The principal had been as kind and understanding as he could have hoped for, but she was obliged to inform their parents that they had threatened a teacher. A telling-off was in store when they got home that afternoon.

Flynn wished they could all be in the same classroom, but he, Briar, and Paddy were all a year apart, which meant different year levels. He couldn't for the life of him figure out why that was necessary. Learning certainly wasn't done separately at home.

"I guess I'll see you two at lunch," he said, spotting his classroom.

"Have fun," said Briar.

Paddy said nothing, but simply turned and walked away.

Flynn forced his brother's dark mood from his mind and climbed the steps to the classroom. Should he knock? He decided against it.

He took a deep breath and pushed the door open.

Instead of silence and curious stares, Flynn found the complete opposite. The class was in a state of high excitement, and the few children who noticed his entrance simply looked at him for a moment and then completely ignored him.

Standing at the front of classroom was his teacher, who he knew was called Mrs McAlpine. She had her back to him, and was busy drawing on the whiteboard.

"Smoke!" yelled one of the children.

"Of course," she replied, and her hand moved rapidly as she drew.

"An arrowhead tail," called out another.

"Got it," replied Mrs McAlpine.

She turned to face the class, stepping away from the whiteboard. Then she caught sight of Flynn standing in the doorway.

"Oh, hello," she said, smiling at him. Flynn could see past her to the whiteboard, and what she'd been drawing on it: a dragon. It was bright green, like the one they had all seen on the billboard: his poor Elton.

"You must be Flynn," she continued. "Welcome to Room 9. You're just in time. We're imagining our own dragon – before we get to see the real thing. We're going to see how accurately we can do it, then compare after we've been to Dragon World. What do you think? Have you ever seen a dragon? Have we missed anything?"

Flynn simply stood there, speechless.

Finally, he found his voice. "I… I… I've never seen one," he said.

Mrs McAlpine smiled again.

"Of course you haven't," she said. "No one has."

Paddy, meanwhile, had been ordered to sit down and shut up by the very same teacher they had threatened only half an hour before. He couldn't believe his terrible luck that he had been assigned to this class! Mr Strickland ran a truly miserable classroom, his students sitting unmoving in orderly rows facing the whiteboard, and only permitted to speak when spoken to. He stood at the front and droned on and on about something called algebra. Paddy did try to concentrate but couldn't manage it. He was tormented with worry about the dragons, and what would become of them at Dragon World. He racked his brains, trying to think of something he could do, but could come up with nothing. He'd never felt so powerless.

As Paddy's thoughts churned in fruitless, frustrating circles, he became aware of a faint but constant scratching from the neighbouring desk. Sitting at it was a girl. She was leaning forward, and her dark hair hung down, hiding her face. Paddy could see she was sketching something on a scrap of paper, her pencil moving rapidly. He tried to see what it was without being too obvious, but her other hand shielded the picture. She, too, ignored Mr Strickland and his boring lesson.

Finally, she completed what she was drawing, and sat back to admire it, moving her hands away. Paddy caught a glimpse, and what he saw made him gasp. She had drawn a dragon, uncomfortably imprisoned in a cage. Its expressive features showed it was terribly sad. The girl was clearly a talented artist. But what struck Paddy most of all were the words written above the picture: 'Dragons aren't meant to live in cages. SET THEM FREE!'

"I said take out some paper, a pencil, a calculator and a highlighter!"

Paddy was jolted from his thoughts by Mr Strickland, who was standing before him. The teacher thumped his fist down on Paddy's desk, and thrust forward his face.

"WAKE UP, BOY!" he bellowed. Paddy could smell his awful breath.

Hurriedly he reached into his bag, and grabbed a pad and the stub of a pencil, placing them before him on his desk.

"Where's your calculator?" hissed Mr Strickland.

"Um… what's a calculator?" said Paddy.

"Are you trying to be funny, boy?"

"And a highlighter?" said Paddy. "I don't know what that is."

Laughter rang out around the classroom. Paddy hung his head. But he could see, out of the corner of his eye, the girl beside him. She was looking right at him, and she wasn't laughing.

By noon, Paddy had had enough. He was bored listening to Mr Strickland, who had moved on to teach science. He'd spent the past half-hour talking about the producer-predator life cycle. Some animals eat grass, other animals eat those animals. To Paddy, it was like saying that the sky was blue and the sea was wet. Everything he said was so obvious that surely it didn't need explaining?

Paddy pushed back his chair and rose to his feet. He stretched. He couldn't remember ever sitting still for so long. He felt sleepy and sluggish, and needed some fresh air. Turning, he walked towards the door.

"Where do you think you're going?"

Mr Strickland's voice rose across the classroom.

Paddy stopped. "Outside," he replied.

"What do you mean, outside?"

Paddy was confused.

"I mean through that door. I'm going to spend some time on the other side of that door."

Mr Strickland looked stunned. His face reddened and he spluttered in disbelief.

"What!? You can't just leave! Who do you think you are?"

"I can't leave? Why not?" Paddy asked.

Again, he caught the dark-haired girl staring at him curiously. "You mean, we have to stay here all the time?"

Mr Strickland exploded. "To the principal's office! Now!"

# CHAPTER 6

Paddy was furious. It was all so unfair. He ran down the steps from the principal's office – where he'd received a second telling-off – and out into the playground. The children were sitting in groups, eating their lunch, but he had no interest in talking to any of them. Instead, he ran to the centre of the schoolyard, to a tall structure he'd heard kids calling the 'jungle gym'. He had no idea what that meant, but it looked like the perfect place to work off some of his frustration.

There were ropes and poles, ladders and climbing walls, bars and swings. He leaped up into them, swinging through them like a monkey. It felt good to use his muscles. He worked his way up to the top of the jungle gym, leaping from beam to beam and swinging his body with abandon. He let go of ropes and flew through the air, catching onto bars. When he reached the top he stood up on the highest bar, balancing with his arms outstretched. Below and ten feet away was a steel ladder, mounted horizontally between two towers. He eyed it, then crouched down on the bar and without hesitation leaped for it, sailing through the air. Grasping the ladder, he used the momentum of his body to swing his legs beneath him then let go again, somersaulting backwards.

Upside down, Paddy spotted his landing and brought his feet through to hit the wooden beam at the edge of the jungle gym. He landed on it squarely but wobbled – it would have been easier in bare feet – but he kept his balance, then dropped lightly to the ground.

It was a few moments before he noticed the silence. Then it struck him, and he looked over at the children gathered around the edge of the schoolyard. They were no longer eating their lunch, but seemed to be frozen in time, sandwiches halfway to their mouths. Every last kid in the school was staring at him, mouths agape.

Paddy ran. He cut across the schoolyard and ducked down an alleyway between classrooms. Slipping around the back of one of them, he found a little corner in the sunshine, out of sight of anyone coming up the path. He sat down and drew his knees up to his chest. He was breathing heavily, more from embarrassment than from his exertions. He cursed himself for drawing so much attention, but he had needed to do something physical, to rid himself of the frustration he felt. He forced himself to take long, slow breaths and closed his eyes. Finally, he began to relax.

"Only halfway through your first day, and already you've been sent to the principal's office twice. That's got to be some sort of record."

Paddy looked up, squinting into the bright sunshine. It was the girl from the classroom. She was taller than he'd realised, and looked strong and athletic. She smiled at him.

"Reckon you'll make it through the afternoon?"

"You mean we have to go back in there?" asked Paddy.

The girl laughed. "Where are you from? Outer space? Of course we do."

Paddy groaned. "For how long?"

"Are you kidding me? Have you never been to school before? Until 3pm."

Paddy looked up at the sun, gauging the time. He guessed it was almost 1pm. Two more hours of Mr Strickland! He put his head in his hands.

"Relax," said the girl, sitting down beside him. "We have another half-hour of lunch yet."

Their backs were to the classroom wall, and she closed her eyes, enjoying the sunshine.

"I'm Beth," she said. She didn't open her eyes. It was as if she was talking to herself.

"Paddy," he replied. He liked that she didn't look at him, and didn't seem to be too bothered about whether or not he spoke. But he realised he was thankful for her company. He felt isolated and lonely, and couldn't shake the anger that boiled up inside him whenever he spoke to his brother or Briar. Earlier he had spotted them across the other side of the playground. A dozen kids were gathered around them, all talking excitedly.

"Nice to meet you," murmured Beth.

Paddy was silent for a while, but then he had to ask.

"You don't agree with Dragon World?"

"Ah. You saw my picture." She smiled, her eyes still closed.

"Yes."

"Well, the truth is I don't believe there are any dragons. The Dragon World stadium is owned by a criminal – The Pitbull. Everyone in this city knows he's a crook, but no one can prove it. And he's dangerous – no one dares speak out against him.

I think he's trying to pull the biggest scam in history, and he's going to steal everyone's money. I think he's made the whole thing up."

"The dragons are real," replied Paddy quietly.

Beth turned to him, opening her eyes, which flashed with sudden anger.

"You sound just like the rest of the kids at this school. You believe they are, and you take the word of a criminal, only because you want to believe it. You want dragons to be real. Well, I think that's stupid. I don't think they are."

"Then why are you drawing posters saying they should be free?"

Beth smiled, and sat back against the wall.

"Just in case," she said.

Paddy was quiet for a while. He wanted to tell her she was wrong, but knew he couldn't do that without telling her how he knew. And if he did, she might not believe him, and just laugh at him. He didn't know anything about her. He didn't know if she could be trusted. And what was the point in telling her anyway? She was just a kid, like him, powerless to do anything about Dragon World.

Just as Paddy was coming to this conclusion, he found himself speaking.

"I know they're real because I've seen them," he said.

"Oh please..." Beth began, but when she glanced at him she fell silent.

He was full of emotion, fighting back tears. He spoke rapidly, telling her everything. It tumbled out of him like a waterfall. He told her about The Island, about the dragons that lived there, and how he'd ridden on their backs just like people ride horses. He told her about the volcano, the earthquakes and the tsunami, about how they'd been forced to leave. And, finally, he told her about The Pitbull capturing The Island's entire population of dragons. For some reason, he left out the part about Briar's treachery.

Finally, he stopped talking, regretting what he'd done. He shouldn't have told her anything.

Beth looked stunned. She stared at him, speechless. Paddy couldn't tell what she was thinking.

Just as she finally found her voice, the bell rang for the end of the lunch break. But Paddy heard what she said, quietly, almost to herself.

"We have to free them."

# CHAPTER 7

The entire staff of Dragon World was gathered in The Pitbull's boardroom. The more senior managers sat around the huge, black oval table with the picture of a dog's head inlaid into its centre in white marble. The rest of them stood around the room, packed like sardines into every available space. It was hot and stuffy.

The Pitbull had ordered them all here to go through the plans for the countdown to the grand opening of Dragon World. Nothing could be left to chance. There was much to do, and less than five days in which to do it!

"From now on, you are all to stay here," began The Pitbull. "You cannot go home tonight, or any night until the grand opening, or leave at any time during the day. Beds will be set up for you in the corridors."

A chorus of protest rose from the staff. "But I have a wife and children to look after!" protested a middle-aged man in a suit towards the head of the table. "You can't possibly keep us here – it's against the law!"

The Pitbull looked at him coolly. He briefly tried to remember what this man did for him, then decided he didn't care. Instead, he smiled.

"In here, I am the law," he replied. "Do you understand?"

There was a long silence. The man's jaw worked, but he kept his mouth shut.

"I thought so," said The Pitbull. "Now shut up and listen."

The Pitbull went through all the details of what he wanted done, and followed them up with threats of what would happen if the staff didn't follow his orders to the letter. By the time he had finished, he could see they were all terrified of messing up, which was just how he liked it. He didn't allow them to ask any questions, but simply dismissed them from the room.

The Pitbull then picked up the phone and dialled his lawyer.

"Has the court order been delivered?" he asked.

"Yes, sir. The police handed it directly to the father at noon today."

He nodded, satisfied. It was always best to hit someone when they were down.

His thoughts were interrupted by a knock at the door.

"Sir? Sir?" came a timid voice.

"What?" barked The Pitbull.

"Sir, the director is here. Your TV advertisement is finished. He wants to show it to you."

The Pitbull rubbed his hands together. He'd been looking forward to seeing himself on screen.

"What are you waiting for? Send him in. Hurry up!"

The door opened and the pathetic director was pushed in, a laptop in his hand and the stupid beret still on his head.

"Hello again, sir," he began, but The Pitbull held up a hand to silence him. He had no wish to listen to the man's nonsense.

"Just play the ad," he commanded.

The director flipped open his laptop and pressed play.

The Pitbull's face loomed out of the black screen. He looked handsome, moody, and mysterious. It was perfect.

"Soon, everything you thought you knew about the animal kingdom will be proved wrong," he heard himself say on screen. His voice sounded rich, deep, commanding. "Myth will become legend, and fantasy become fact!"

The Pitbull's sense of excitement grew as he watched the advertisement. Dragon World was almost here! He was about to become the most famous man in the world!

The on-screen version of himself was getting ready for his big reveal.

"That something… was the presence, the very existence, of dragons! Real, fire-breathing dragons!" he said, and the camera zoomed back.

Instantly, The Pitbull knew this advertisement wasn't going to work. The huge green dragon beneath his foot didn't look real at all. It didn't just look dead, it looked like it was made of plastic. He silently cursed his men for giving it so much tranquilliser. Apparently it had recovered later, but in this advertisement it simply looked like a fake.

Beside him, the director shifted uncomfortably in his seat.

"There is another version, sir," he mumbled. "One without the dragon. It's just you talking to the camera for the whole thing. It's very good, sir."

The Pitbull considered for a moment. He really did look very handsome and powerful on screen.

It was good enough for the public – it was more than good enough. It was amazing. The dragon really wasn't that important. He was the main event, when you really thought about it.

"Put the version without the dragon on TV," he ordered. "From tonight. Have them play it every hour of every day until opening night."

Here's your first opportunity to use the **AR Reads** app on your device (if you haven't downloaded it, find out how at the beginning of this book. If you have, make sure it's the latest version).

Simply start up the app, then point the device at this page and check out The Pitbull's advertisement for Dragon World! If you don't have a device – don't worry – just read on!

# CHAPTER 8

B riar's thoughts wavered between despair about the dragons and guilt that she'd actually enjoyed her first day of school. Some of the kids had been lovely to her and Flynn, and she'd found herself laughing more than once, despite her sadness. It took some adjustment, sitting in a classroom for so long after the freedom of her life on The Island, but she was sure she and Flynn would get used to it.

But poor Paddy was a different story. He seemed to have sunk even deeper into his black mood.

He trailed well behind Briar and Flynn, walking slowly, looking down at his feet. He seemed not to even hear when they called out to him, let alone answer. Once again, they gave up trying, leaving him to walk home alone. Briar could see Flynn was upset, and nothing she said seemed to cheer him up.

As Briar walked through the gates of their home, she bumped into Flynn. He'd stopped on the path, and was looking up at his father, who sat on the top step, obviously waiting for them. He had a strange expression on his face. In his hand was a sheet of paper.

"What is it, Dad?" asked Flynn. He ran up the stairs two at a time. "What's the matter?"

Briar felt her stomach twist and leap. Flynn's father was ashen, the colour drained from his face. He was looking right at her.

"Briar," he said. "I... I... don't know how to tell you this." His voice trailed away.

"What, Dad?" cried Flynn. "Tell us!"

Flynn's father swallowed hard. He looked at Briar.

"Your uncle wants you back. The police delivered this court order here today." He held out the paper.

Briar couldn't speak. She felt like she couldn't even breathe.

"What's a court order, Dad?" asked Flynn, grabbing it from him.

"It's… it's… it means that Briar has to go back to live with The Pitbull or we'll be arrested and charged with kidnapping."

"They can't do that!" Flynn exploded.

"I'm afraid they can," replied his father sadly. "It's the law. We have no legal right to keep Briar with us. We haven't adopted her, and I don't think The Pitbull would ever let us. We'll fight it – your mother is already trying to find a lawyer – but it will be very difficult."

Just then Paddy walked in through the gate. He stopped, looking first at his father, then at Flynn and Briar.

"What's happened?"

Flynn and his father explained the court order

to Paddy, who listened in silence. When they were finished, he turned to Briar.

"Just as you planned, huh? Now you get to go home again. Well done, Briar." He walked straight past her into the house.

Briar was stunned, but her shock quickly hardened to anger.

"That's it," she said grimly, before following Paddy into the house. Flynn hurried along behind her.

Paddy was sitting on his bed in the brothers' room, and he looked up in surprise as Briar marched right in. Flynn stayed well back in the hallway, saying nothing.

"Say it again," said Briar. Her voice didn't sound like her own.

Paddy looked down and busied himself emptying his school bag, and ignoring her.

"SAY IT AGAIN!" yelled Briar.

This time Paddy couldn't ignore her.

"Say what again?"

"Accuse me one more time of helping my uncle catch the dragons. Accuse me again of planning this all along. See what happens. GO ON! I DARE YOU!" she yelled at him.

"Get out of my room," he said. His voice was thick with emotion.

"SAY IT!" Briar screamed.

Paddy didn't say a word, but simply stood up and tried to walk out of the room. Briar blocked the door.

"Oh no, you don't," she said. "You don't get to say that to me and just walk away. We're having this out, right now."

Paddy sat down on the bed again.

"Don't be a child," he said quietly.

"Me?" said Briar. She laughed in disbelief. "Me? I'm behaving like a child? It's you who's the baby. You've been absolutely awful since we left The Island! And I understand that you want someone to blame, but it's not me! And don't you ever accuse me again!" Briar's voice cracked, and she wiped away a tear. But she wasn't about to leave Paddy in any doubt.

"You're selfish, and you're mean! You're feeling sorry for yourself and taking it out on everyone else.

You don't know how lucky you are, getting to stay here with your wonderful family, while I have to go back to live with my uncle!"

Briar turned to leave, and Flynn stood back as she walked past him. She didn't want to let Paddy know she was crying, but she couldn't stifle a sob. She went into the room she shared with Ada and slammed the door.

Half an hour later, there was a knock.

"Briar?" It was the boys' mother.

"Come in."

She entered, her face full of concern.

"Is there no way we can stop it?" Briar asked.

"We'll try, sweetheart, but I don't think so, not right now. But even if you have to go, we won't give up. We'll fight this until we get you back, one way or another."

Briar hung her head. "When do I have to go?"

"The Pitbull wants you delivered to Dragon World on opening night, two hours before the show starts. The policeman said he'd be left with no choice but to arrest us if you don't show up."

# CHAPTER 9

When Flynn woke the following morning it was still dark outside, but try as he might he couldn't get back to sleep. His thoughts were in turmoil. He felt like he was trapped in a maze – every time he tried to figure out a solution to one of half a dozen problems, he hit a dead end. He looked over at his brother, who was silent. Flynn couldn't tell if he was awake or asleep.

Briar had gone to bed without dinner, and Paddy stayed in his room too. Flynn had sat with his mother and father and grandparents, who all tried to console him but even they struggled to find anything positive to say.

He just wished they could be back on The Island. Everything had been so good, so fun, and Briar had brought something new to all of their lives. And in four days she would be gone again. How could it have all gone so wrong, so quickly?

Flynn rolled out of bed and quietly padded to the kitchen. To his surprise his grandparents were already up.

"Good morning," said Roger, winking at him.

Millicent kissed him on the forehead.

"You're up early."

"So are you," Flynn replied, and then he saw, piled by the door, two large gear bags and some food packed into a box. "What are you two up to? Are you leaving?"

His grandfather nodded. "We're off adventuring. It's a bit cramped here in the house, so your grandmother and I thought we'd take a little trip."

"Where?" asked Flynn suspiciously.

"Don't know exactly," said Roger. "We'll see where the wind takes us."

"You're going on the yacht? Where?"

Roger chuckled. "I've heard there are some lovely little bays north of here that are full of fish just waiting for me to cast a line at them. Maybe we'll pay them a visit."

Flynn looked at his grandmother, who smiled.

"It'll only be for a few weeks – three at the most," she said.

Roger rose from the table and poured the remains of his tea down the sink. "We'd better go, my love," he said. "Time and tide wait for no man – or woman."

Roger picked up the bags, and Flynn brought the box of food out to their dusty old car. He loaded it into the boot.

"Give me a hug," said Millicent.

Flynn closed his eyes as he hugged his grandmother. He was used to their coming and going – without fail they had visited The Island on the full moon each month – but this time it was strange.

It was topsy-turvy. It was they who were heading for the wilderness, while he remained in the city, trapped.

"Be patient with your brother," said Roger. "Give him time. He'll come around eventually. He's just finding a way to deal with it all."

Flynn nodded, and hugged his grandfather.

"I will. Be careful."

Flynn stood on the side of the road until his grandparents' car disappeared around the corner.

When he went back inside Paddy was just emerging from their bedroom. He looked dog-tired, like he'd barely slept. His hair stuck up all over his head.

They ate breakfast together, not speaking. Flynn remembered what his grandfather had said. Give Paddy time. In the silence, the sound of Flynn munching his toast was amplified. He'd burned it – he loved toast but hadn't yet mastered using a toaster – and every mouthful he took crunched loudly.

Flynn took another bite and Paddy looked at him. Flynn thought he could detect a twinkle in his brother's eyes.

Very slowly, and holding eye contact with Paddy, Flynn raised his toast to his mouth. He opened his mouth wide, baring his teeth. Then, very slowly he sank them into the slice of toast. It made a ridiculously loud crunch.

Paddy couldn't help himself. He began to giggle. Then Flynn did too. Pretty soon both of them were helpless with laughter. Paddy fell backwards off his stool, which made them laugh even more. It was so good to see Paddy laughing again that Flynn forgot all his troubles for the moment.

Neither of them noticed Briar come into the kitchen until she was standing over them, hands on her hips. Flynn saw immediately that she'd been crying. Her eyes were red and she clutched a tissue.

The brothers fell silent. Paddy lay on his back on the floor, looking up at Briar.

"I'm sorry," he said. "I've been an idiot."

Briar nodded. "You have. But it's OK."

"No, it's not," said Paddy, sitting up. "I always believed what you were saying, but I think it was easier to be angry with you, to blame everything on you. Can you forgive me?"

Briar smiled at him. "We'll see," she said.

Briar sat down at the table. Paddy picked himself up off the floor.

"What are we going to do about the court order from The Pitbull?" he asked.

"Right now? Absolutely nothing," said Briar. "I don't want to think about it. I just want to have breakfast like it's a normal day. What were you two laughing about, anyway?"

"Well," said Flynn, picking up the remaining corner of his toast, "let me show you."


An hour later the children left the house for school. They were laughing and messing about, chasing each other up the street.

The boys' mother watched them go, thankful that Paddy and Briar had settled their differences. But the dark cloud of the court order would not lift. At the end of the week Briar – lovely, kind, sweet Briar – would have to be delivered, like a parcel in the mail, back to The Pitbull. There was nothing anyone could do about it.

She turned and walked back inside with a heavy heart. She heard the television in the lounge – her husband had turned it on to watch the morning news – and went in to look. On the screen was an evil-looking man with a nasty scar running down the right-hand side of his face. He was speaking directly to the camera, but with the sound low she couldn't quite hear what he was saying.

Her husband was in the armchair, and when he heard her come in he turned to her. She immediately saw that all colour had drained from his face.

"What is it?" she asked, panicked by his expression.

He pointed at the screen. "It's an advertisement for Dragon World. And that man…" he began. "That man… he's The Pitbull. I recognise him… I knew him – a long time ago."

# CHAPTER 10

As soon as the children turned into the street Paddy spotted it. In fact, there was no way anyone could miss it. A huge sign, apparently made from a bed sheet, and painted with thick black lettering, had been tied to the fence that surrounded their school. As they got closer, the children could see that there were two more of them on other parts of the fence.

The first sign read simply: 'No to Dragon World'. The second said 'Dragons are wild animals – they belong in the wild!' and on the third was written: 'Free the dragons, lock up The Pitbull!'

Paddy felt his heart start to thump harder in his chest. Who had done this?

Then he saw who. Emerging from the school gates, with yet another sign – this one a large placard on a pole – was his new friend Beth. Emblazoned on her placard was a beautifully drawn picture of a dragon – which looked uncannily like Elton, thought Paddy – and the words 'You're paying for this creature's prison'.

Paddy ran up to her, followed closely by Flynn and Briar.

"Beth! This is amazing," he said. "Why didn't you tell me you were going to do it?"

Beth smiled. "I only decided when I woke up this morning. I opened the curtains and the first thing I saw was a plane towing a banner for Dragon World across the sky, and I decided I had to do something. So here I am. It's not going that well, to be honest."

Paddy looked at the children filing past them, walking into the school grounds. Most of them scowled at Beth. Some muttered under their breath. It was clear that few, if any of them, shared her views.

"We'll stand with you," said Flynn suddenly, stepping forward. "My brother's forgotten his manners. I'm Flynn, and this is Briar, and we're totally with you."

A screech of brakes made them all look up. A van skidded to a halt across the road from the school. Emblazoned on its side were the words *Screentime News*. The door flew open and out

~ 73 ~

tumbled a cameraman and a reporter. The man with the camera went to work immediately, filming the big signs that Beth had made, while the reporter made a beeline for Beth, jogging across the road with his long microphone extended before him like a lance in a jousting match. Paddy couldn't understand why they were in such a hurry, but suddenly another van turned up, and then a third. All were from different TV stations.

"Miss! Miss!" yelled the reporter. "Bob Harrington from Screentime News. Can I ask you a few questions? What's your name? What's your problem with Dragon World?"

Paddy's first reaction was to get away from them all, but to his surprise Beth stepped forward. The journalist was joined by his cameraman, who pointed his giant camera right at Beth's face. The two other news crews raced across the road and stood close behind them. Beth was unperturbed. She answered all their questions confidently and thoughtfully.

But the journalists were scornful of her, and it made Paddy furious. To his surprise, the plucky girl kept her cool, looking into the camera and telling everyone who'd bought a ticket to Dragon World not to use it. Finally, she told the news crews that she was late for school and walked away.

Paddy ran to catch up with Beth.

"That was awesome," he said. "Do you think it will work?"

Beth shook her head. "Not a chance. People will still go. We have to do something else."

# CHAPTER 11

"We're ready for the rehearsal," came the voice through the intercom.

"Bulb, rise," ordered The Pitbull.

The Pitbull heard the hum of hydraulics beneath him and the room began to rise, so smoothly it was almost imperceptible. He felt a rush of pride.

As the bulb rose up out of the ground, with him inside it, the entire stadium came into view. It was almost dark, with just a faint orange glow in the sky. Everything seemed in order. Where the sports field had been, there was now a dramatic rocky landscape.

He hoped that the dragons would arrange themselves around it, settling on huge boulders where the audience could appreciate their awesome majesty.

The rocks were all fake, built of steel and plaster and painted to look like stone, but you couldn't tell. At one end of the arena was a waterfall, which cascaded thirty feet from the highest rock into a crystal-clear pond. It had cost an absolute fortune, that waterfall. All manner of filters and pumps had to be installed to make it work, but it had been worth it. As if on cue, a large salmon leaped clear of the water and landed with a splash. The Pitbull saw it through the imagined eyes of a thrilled audience, and his heart leaped right along with it.

Higher and higher rose the bulb. From here he could just make out the outlines of the trapdoors through which the dragons would emerge into the arena. They had been cleverly disguised as part of the floor. The audience would never expect it.

He looked up and around the stadium at the giant mirror balls, lights and lasers, water and fire cannons

Here's your second opportunity to use the **AR Reads** app on your device.

Simply start up the app, then point the device at this page and check out the arena and The Pitbull's bulb. If you don't have a device – don't worry – just read on!

and row upon row of speakers. Giant steel bars, coated with a heatproof substance called hafnium, crisscrossed the roof and separated the audience from the dragons.

The bulb juddered to a halt thirty metres above the arena. It swayed ever so slightly, and The Pitbull gripped the podium to steady himself.

A voice came through the intercom. "Ready when you are, sir."

The Pitbull smiled. "Start the smoke machines," he ordered.

Four huge jets of dry ice smoke immediately began to pour from unseen pipes and spread across the arena floor.

"More!" commanded The Pitbull. The control tower responded with an impressive amount, but it was still not enough. "Install more pipes. I want a thick carpet of smoke," he said.

"Yes, sir," came the reply. "The PA is all systems go. Just push the blue button on the microphone and you're live, sir."

The Pitbull pushed the button, and immediately heard the electrostatic hum of the speakers resonate through the glass of the bulb.

"Ladies and gentlemen," he began, and then stopped in wonder. "Gentlemen, gentlemen, gentlemen..." his voice echoed around the vast empty stadium. The power of the speakers was incredible. It put a broad grin on his face. "I want to congratulate you all on your decision to purchase a ticket to Dragon World. Because you are about to see one of the natural wonders of the world, in the GREATEST SHOW ON EARTH!

The Pitbull pumped his fist with excitement. He tapped on the intercom.

"Cages, open. Trapdoors, open," he commanded.

Through the dry ice smoke he saw the trapdoors fly open, leaving a yawning black hole in the ground. He peered at it, but could see nothing. No dragons flew out of it. Ten seconds went by, then twenty.

"What's happening?" he barked into the intercom.

"Sir, the dragons won't budge. They won't leave their cages," came the reply.

"Then use the hoses, you idiots! That's what they're for!"

"Yes, sir."

His eyes glued to the trapdoors, he waited another fifteen seconds. No dragons flew out.
The intercom crackled into life.

"Sir, you have to give the order, sir. It's operated by your voice only, sir."

The Pitbull stamped his foot in frustration.

"Oh for heaven's sake! Hoses, on!" he bellowed.

He heard the shouts of men through the intercom, and then the sound of gushing water. A hundred huge nozzles had been installed all around the room full of cages, and they could spray jets of water to any part with such force no creature would stand it for long. They pumped out so much water the room would be completely filled in less than half a minute.

Another ten seconds went by, and just as The Pitbull was beginning to think they'd have to go back to the drawing board and figure out some other way to get the lazy animals moving, a single dragon shot up out of the opening and into the arena. It rose vertically to the roof, before flattening out just below the steel bars. Then another flew out of the hole, followed by a third, then a fourth. Suddenly, all of the dragons burst out in a torrent. The air vibrated with the claps of their beating wings and their ferocious, angry roars. They rose in a great cloud, and finding themselves imprisoned, they began to fly in circles, like a huge, multi-coloured tornado. At the centre of it all was the glass bulb, with The Pitbull inside. He gasped at the spectacle. He couldn't speak. It was fearsome, and awesome. His heart beat like a bass drum in his chest. It was more incredible, more jaw-droppingly astounding, than he could ever have imagined.

"The lasers!" he yelled. "Start the lasers – and the strobe light!"

Immediately, every one of the high-powered laser lights went on, sending coloured beams of light piercing through the smoke of the dry ice machines. Then the strobe light kicked in, flickering on and off fifteen times a second. It was intensely powerful, and the effect was to double or triple the apparent number of dragons whirling through the air.

"Oh my," whispered The Pitbull. He felt weak, and giddy with excitement at the same time. He could hardly believe his eyes.

*Thwack!* Something hit the bulb hard, making it shudder and sway at the top of its pole. He looked around but could see nothing. He gripped the podium. The movement of the dragons had lifted the dry ice from the stadium floor and up into the air above the arena. It was difficult to see anything. The strobe light picked out the speeding dragons, but they were moving so fast they disappeared in the mist before he could focus on them. The odd collision with the bulb was bound to happen now and again with all the smoke and light, he reasoned, but he knew how strong the glass was and he wasn't particularly worried.

*Slam!* Again the bulb shuddered under a glancing blow, and this time The Pitbull saw the dragon – a canary-yellow female. It flapped off into the darkness. But in the instant before it disappeared, it seemed to be looking directly at him. His blood ran cold.

*BOOM!* A dragon hit the bulb so hard The Pitbull was thrown to the ground under the impact. The glass held firm, but he landed so violently his head whiplashed into the steel floor of the bulb. It made his vision blur, but when it cleared he found himself looking straight up into the furious eyes of an enormous green male dragon. It was the same beast he'd had tranquillised for the advertisement, he was sure of it. It perched on the roof of the bulb, staring straight down at The Pitbull with an intensity that made him curl up on the ground. As he cowered in terror, he saw the dragon open its mouth and send forth a white-hot river of fire directly at the bulb.

The Pitbull remembered his engineers assuring him that the bulb was heatproof, but it was clear they hadn't figured on this level of intensity. The temperature inside was rising by the second.

*WHACK!* Another dragon struck the bulb, and again it swayed violently atop its pole. The Pitbull yelped and curled up into a tight ball. When he dared to look he saw that this dragon was blue. It was clinging to the pole underneath the bulb, so he could only see its head and one of its yellow wings. It, too, stared right at him. The laser lights made its scales sparkle like sapphires, but The Pitbull couldn't appreciate it because he was frightened out of his wits. The blue dragon suddenly sent forth a jet of fire of its own. The temperature rose even higher.

An awful screech from above made The Pitbull whimper, and he was horrified to see that the green terror overhead was dragging its hideous talons down the side of the bulb. There was no doubt he was trying to get in.

"Down!" he screamed. "Bulb, down!"

Immediately the bulb began to move, but both dragons were now attempting to tear at its surface, while superheating it with white-hot rivers of fire. The heat inside would soon become unbearable.

"Faster!" he bellowed. "Get me out of here!"

"It can't go any faster," came the reply, and The Pitbull vowed to fire whoever was on the other end of the intercom.

Suddenly, he had an idea.

"Water!" he yelled. "The hoses! Turn them on the bulb!"

An agonising few seconds ticked by, while steadily the heat rose. He scrambled to the centre of the bulb, as far from the glass as he could get. Then, suddenly, thankfully, a thunderous torrent of water from the huge firehoses mounted to the stadium roof struck the bulb from all sides. Both dragons were immediately blasted off and flapped away into the darkness. Clouds of steam billowed upwards, accompanied by a fierce hissing. Fearfully, The Pitbull scanned the glass for cracks, but couldn't see any. As the bulb was finally lowered into the ground, he lay back on the floor in sheer relief.

He began to cry, and sobbed pitifully for a long time. He didn't notice the doors to the bulb opening, nor realise that he was being observed by one of his men. Finally, the man coughed uncomfortably, and The Pitbull scrabbled to his feet in shame, turning his back to him.

"Ah… that went well, sir," said the man. "The dragons don't like the hoses at all. As soon as we started to spray them in the arena they all went back down to their cages. They're in there now, safe and sound. The bulb appears to be undamaged too, sir."

"You're fired," said The Pitbull.

"Yes, sir," the man replied. "But before I go, sir, I should tell you that there's someone here to see you, sir. He's waiting in the lobby."

# CHAPTER 12

As soon as the bell rang for lunch, Flynn, Paddy, Briar, and Beth gathered on the school field in the shade of a large oak tree. The two girls were deep in conversation and the boys sat quietly by, listening and eating their lunch. Beth told Briar all about her life – how she had been adopted when she was a baby, and how her adoptive parents had then changed their minds, giving her up to an orphanage. From there she had gone through a series of foster parents, never spending more than a year with any of them. Currently she was living with an awful couple – cruel and heartless – who didn't seem to care if she was there or not.

"I think the only reason they have me is so they can get the money from the government for my care," she explained.

Paddy felt selfish, realising that during their conversation behind the classroom he hadn't asked Beth anything about herself. As she continued her story, he learned that she had no brothers or sisters, and had never found out who her real parents were.

"It must have been so lonely for you," said Briar, a look of deep concern on her face.

"It was, I guess," said Beth. "But I learned to get on with it. I'm so independent now. I realised pretty early on that the only person I could truly rely on was me."

Paddy spoke up. "Not anymore."

Beth smiled. "Thanks. That means a lot."

Next it was Briar's turn. She told Beth all about her uncle The Pitbull, and how she came to live with him. When she spoke about losing her parents, the girls hugged for a long time, fighting back tears.

Although Paddy had heard the story many times, it still made him emotional too. When Briar finished her story with the news about the court order and having to return to live with The Pitbull, Beth gasped.

"Oh no!" she cried. "You can't possibly go back to him!"

"I have to," said Briar. "The police will arrest Flynn and Paddy's parents if I don't. I can't let that happen."

Beth fell silent. She had a habit of chewing on her lower lip when she was thinking, and she was doing it now.

"What if we all left the house?" asked Paddy. "Perhaps we could find somewhere else to live – where the police won't find us?"

"We might be able to hide for a while, but not forever," said Flynn. "Then Mum and Dad would be in even more trouble."

"Flynn's right," said Beth. She chewed on her lip some more. "I know this sounds crazy, but maybe Briar going back to her uncle is a good thing."

Paddy turned to her in disbelief. "How can you say that? He's horrible to her!"

Beth put up her hands. "Wait – hear me out. If we're to stop Dragon World somehow, it's going to help a whole lot if we have someone on the inside."

A grin spread across Briar's face. Her eyes flashed with determination.

"Beth's right," she said. "I'll do whatever I can."

Beth rummaged in her bag and pulled out a slim, rectangular case. On the top was a sort of silver badge, which looked like an apple with a bite taken out of it. Paddy had no idea what it was. She flipped up the lid, revealing rows of buttons covered with letters and numbers, and a screen. When she tapped a button, the screen lit up.

"What's that?" marvelled Paddy.

Beth laughed. "Oh boy, you guys crack me up. It's my laptop. It's a computer. It took me years to save up for this."

Paddy thought it looked like some sort of glowing book.

Beth continued. "I set up some social media accounts for people who want to help stop Dragon World," she said, sliding her finger over a small pad beside the buttons and clicking rapidly. "Let's see how they're going."

Paddy had no idea what Beth was talking about, but he and the others gathered behind her to look at the screen. She flipped through a number of photos, mostly of the signs she had made that morning.

"Wow," said Beth. "We already have over two thousand followers since this morning. That's incredible."

"You mean, all these people agree with you – with us – that Dragon World should be stopped?" said Flynn.

Beth nodded. Her fingers flew rapidly across the keyboard, too fast to even follow what she was doing.

"How did you learn to do this?" Paddy asked.

"I've spent an awful lot of time on my own," replied Beth.

As the children watched, Beth set up an event on all the social media pages she had created. It was a protest, to take place outside the gates of Dragon World, starting at 6pm, an hour before the grand opening was due to begin. With a click the event went live.

"There," she said. "If even half of these people turn up it should make things interesting."

Just then, the school bell pealed out across the field. Children reluctantly began to walk back towards the classrooms.

"Tonight I'll have a good look at the Dragon World website, and see if I can hack into it," said Beth.

Paddy had no idea what Beth was talking about, but he stared at her with awe. He felt a flicker of optimism. He could see by the looks on Flynn and Briar's faces that they felt the same. Beth had given them just what they had needed: a plan of action, and hope.

# CHAPTER 13

As The Pitbull headed for the lobby to meet his visitor he was in a truly foul mood. Leaving the glass bulb and making his way through the cage room, he walked past the guards' station – a tiny office with a heavy, rubber-lined door to keep out the water from the hoses. The door was open, and as he passed he noticed that two of his men were watching TV. He turned on his heel and was about to fire them for being so lazy, but something on the screen made him forget all about that. It was a news flash, and the irritating, excited voice of a reporter was playing over images of home-made signs protesting against Dragon World.

"What the hell is this?" he roared.

"Nothing to worry about, sir. It's just a stupid schoolgirl, sir. She's protesting against Dragon World," replied one of the guards.

"Don't tell me what to worry about!" snapped The Pitbull.

As he watched, the reporter said that several social media accounts started that morning were gaining traction, with supporters from all over the world taking the girl's side.

"Little voices crying in the wilderness," murmured the other guard.

The Pitbull knew his men were right. The protestors were a tiny minority amongst a overwhelming number of supporters of Dragon World. Tickets were now booked out for a full year in advance, and sales showed no sign of slowing.

But still, he couldn't believe that someone had the cheek to stand against him. It made his blood boil.

**SCREENTIME NEWS**

Time to use the **AR Reads** app again!

Simply start up the app, then point the device at this page and see how Beth has made the news. If you don't have a device – don't worry – just read on!

To make himself feel better, he kicked the television clean off the desk. The two guards jumped back, stunned.

The Pitbull knew exactly what to do next. Pulling his phone from his pocket, he dialled the Chief of Police. Before the man even had a chance to speak, The Pitbull snapped an order at him.

"It's me. I want you to arrest the schoolgirl protesting against Dragon World, and if there's any other children helping her arrest them too. Find the reporter – Bob Harrington. Find out what he knows. I want their names, where they live, everything. And I want them locked up – today."

"I'm afraid I can't do that," the Chief stammered. "It's not illegal to stage a peaceful protest."

The Pitbull lowered his voice to a menacing hiss. "I don't care. Make up a reason to charge them. You will arrest them by the end of the day, or face the consequences."

The Pitbull silently gave thanks that he had both threatened the Chief of Police last year, and also sent him on an expensive holiday to Hawaii.

The Chief meekly agreed and hung up, but The Pitbull was boiling inside. He called his head of security and had him send two guards to the school in case the bungling police failed to find the girl.

He was still seething when he arrived in the lobby. The lights were off, and he peered around impatiently, but could see no one. Then, just as he was about to leave, a tall man stepped out of the shadows. He strode across the lobby towards The Pitbull, moving with purpose.

Something about him seemed familiar. The loping stride, the slight tilt of his head. Suddenly, The Pitbull had a flash of recognition. As the man walked out into the light, in his mind The Pitbull travelled back thirty years.

"Do you remember me? We went to school together," said the man.

"I… I… do," said The Pitbull, too surprised to gather his thoughts.

"Flynn and Paddy are my sons," the man continued.

"We live on the island you took the dragons from. Your niece, Briar, lives with us.

We received your court order, but we – my wife and I – want to adopt her, and I'm here to ask your permission for that to happen. If you allow it, you'll never see us again."

The Pitbull began to laugh. He loved it when people pleaded with him. He continued to laugh in the visitor's face – he couldn't even remember his name – until the man turned on his heel and left.

# CHAPTER 14

When the bell rang for the end of school, Flynn, Paddy, Briar, and Beth could hardly wait to get together again. They met in the schoolyard, where immediately they all began talking at once. Flynn had been unable to concentrate on any of his lessons, thinking of nothing but how to stop Dragon World. It was obvious the others felt the same.

"If I'd had to sit through ten more minutes of Mr Strickland's boring class I would have lost my mind," exclaimed Paddy.

Beth grinned. "I think you're driving him crazy too." She turned to Flynn and Briar. "Paddy asked him what a stapler was today."

"OK, that might have been on purpose," said Paddy. "But he deserved it. Oh – look out, here he comes now."

Mr Strickland was striding across the court towards them. He had his mobile phone clutched in his hand.

"Beth, I've got twelve missed calls from the media," he thundered. "They want to know what sort of student you are. You're to take down your stupid signs – now! No one is interested in your opinion."

"Sorry, I can't hear you, Mr Strickland," shouted Beth cheerfully. "Got to go!"

Stifling a giggle, she grabbed the others and they all ran towards the school gates. Behind them, Flynn could hear Mr Strickland ranting and raving.

As the four children rounded the corner of the school office, they came in sight of the school gates.

Beth stopped abruptly, and Flynn almost ran into her. Briar and Paddy skidded to a halt beside him.

"What's up?" Flynn asked, but he didn't need anyone to answer. Outside the school gates there was complete chaos. Hundreds of people stood along the school fence, and on the road, blocking the traffic. Many of them were holding banners and placards and chanting slogans calling for the closure of Dragon World. Others had turned up to shout abuse at the protesters. Panicked parents ran to and fro, trying to find their children amid the crowd. Surrounding all this were at least five news crews and more than a dozen police, who stood stonily watching the proceedings. Flynn also noticed a black car with two men in it parked outside the school. One of them held a large pair of binoculars, which he had trained on the four children. In his other hand he held a phone. As Flynn watched, he dialled a number and put the phone to his ear.

Suddenly, one of the protestors – a woman holding one end of a large banner – spotted Beth.

"There she is!" she yelled, pointing.

A cheer rose from the crowd of protestors, followed by angry jeering from those supporting Dragon World.

"Let's jump over the fence at the back of the school," said Paddy. "No one will see us."

But Beth ignored him. Squaring her shoulders, she marched towards the school gates. Flynn, Paddy, and Briar followed her reluctantly.

Beth stood quietly until the noise of the crowd died down. Then in a clear, high voice, she spoke.

"Thank you for your support. It's most heartening to know that we aren't alone in trying to stop Dragon World. I know you're under pressure protesting against this, and many people don't agree with you, but I urge you all not to give up, and to attend the protest on Saturday. Thank you."

Beth turned and walked away down the footpath, followed by the others. Behind them, a cheer rose up and drowned out the booing and honking of horns from impatient motorists trying to get past.

Paddy and Briar congratulated Beth, but Flynn noticed something that made the hair on his neck stand up. The police were beginning to move towards them, skirting the crowd as they tried to get past. The closest policeman – a tall man in a uniform a few sizes too small for him – was striding towards them rapidly.

"Something's going on," Flynn hissed to the others. "The police are following us. No – don't look back at them. They won't try anything with all these people around, but as soon as we get around the corner be ready to run."

The children did as they were told, keeping their stride steady and trying not to look panicked. The tall policeman was perhaps a hundred feet away, and gaining on them fast. But they were almost at the corner. As soon as they rounded it, and moved into the cover of a thick hedge, Flynn gave the order.

"Run!"

The children took off like greyhounds. Flynn saw that Beth was a natural runner – faster than any of them. By the time he looked back to see the policeman rounding the corner, they'd doubled their lead. He heard the policeman shout, and saw him start in pursuit, and grinned at the man's mistake. He'd never catch them.

The policeman ran for no more than thirty seconds before he realised this too. Flynn saw him stop and reach for his walkie-talkie. He couldn't hear what the man said, but ten seconds later a police car came around the corner in a sideways skid, and screeched to a halt beside him.

"We need to get off the road," puffed Flynn. "Now!"

"Follow me," yelled Paddy. He turned into a driveway and sprinted down the side of a house. The others followed. Flynn hoped no one was home. They were now in the garden, and his brother vaulted the back fence with ease. Briar and Beth followed him over, but before Flynn jumped, he looked back. The police drove up and the doors flew open. Three policemen got out, including the man who'd given chase. They began to sprint after the children.

As soon as Flynn leaped the fence he saw the dog. It was huge – a Rottweiler – and it had been sleeping peacefully in the sun, but was now roused and baring its teeth. Paddy, Briar, and Beth had run past it, and were climbing over the fence on the far side of the yard, but it had seen Flynn, and the hackles rose on its back. Immediately, it flew at Flynn, and he knew he'd never dodge its jaws. He prepared to fight it off.

*CHANK!* The chain around the dog's neck suddenly drew tight, and it was jerked to a halt just a few feet from Flynn. It barked furiously at him, drool flying from its glistening teeth. Flynn's heart pounded in his chest, and he heard his own sigh of relief. He took off again, running in a broad arc to stay out of the dog's reach. Just as he jumped the fence at the far side of the yard, however, he had an idea. But he would have to be quick.

Flynn sprinted along the fence line, and leaped over the corner post into the neighbour's yard. He could now see the three policemen, who had

passed the house and were making for the fence.

The dog had seen them too, and it strained at

the chain, its attention now removed from Flynn.

He didn't have much time. Leaping up on the fence,

he leaned over it, and saw where the nail had been

driven in and bent upwards to attach the dog's chain.

Grabbing it, he pulled with all his might. It bent open

a little, but it was a thick nail, and hard to move.

The dog strained at its collar, and Flynn could see

that each time it lunged, it made the nail flex slightly

in the fencepost. He suddenly saw what to do.

Grabbing the chain, he hauled it up towards the flat head of the nail. It wouldn't pass over the head, but if he could yank at the same time as the dog lunged he might just be able to pull it out of the fence.

The tall policeman got over the fence first. When the dog saw him it went berserk, and ran hard at him. Flynn gripped the nail and waited. At the moment the chain pulled taut, he jerked on the nail with all his strength.

*PING!* The nail flew out of the fencepost and suddenly the dog was loose. It was surprised by its sudden freedom, but it didn't take long to react. It went straight for the policeman, flying at him with a vicious snarl.

Flynn didn't wait to see what would happen next. The panicked shouts and screams of pain from all three men told him enough. He scampered back through the yard and followed his brother and the girls out into the neighbouring street.

# CHAPTER 15

"I know my uncle's behind this!" cried Briar.

The children were huddled under a small bridge, doing their best to keep out of sight of the road. Every now and again a police car would come by, obviously searching for them. They'd also spotted the black car with the two men inside, slowly cruising the streets.

The children had walked a good way along the creek that ran under the bridge, wading through the shallow water, just in case the police had sniffer dogs on their trail. Briar's new-found optimism was fading fast.

"He must be, because it's not against the law for us to protest against Dragon World," said Beth. "Anyone is allowed to do it."

"What are we going to do?" said Briar.

"You definitely can't go home, Beth – the police will be there," said Paddy. "They might be at our place too."

"Paddy's right," agreed Flynn. "We need to make a plan, and we have to stay out of sight. We're as well off here as anywhere for now."

The children sat quietly under the bridge and shared what was left in their lunch boxes. Finally, it began to get dark. They waited until the after-work traffic had died down, then cautiously climbed up the bank onto the road. They'd decided to try to get a message to their parents. None of them could think of anything else to do.

Beth took out her phone and figured out a route that wouldn't take them anywhere near the main roads. They gathered around, staring at the screen in the darkness. She zoomed in on their home with her phone on satellite view.

"If the police are there, they're probably sitting in their vehicles in the streets around your home – perhaps here and here." She pointed at the streets and the likely spots. "They may not be in police cars, either, so we'll have to be very careful."

The children walked quietly through the streets. Briar was comforted by Beth's confidence, but even so she didn't see how they could evade the police. Even if they managed it, she still had to give herself up to her uncle in less than three days' time or else the brothers' parents would be arrested. She couldn't live with herself if that happened!

Flynn suddenly raised a hand to halt them all. Briar had been walking in a daze, lost in her thoughts, and hadn't realised they were so close to the house.

Flynn wordlessly pointed at a black van parked well down on the far side of the road. The streetlights cast an eerie glow over the scene.

The children stood motionless for a long time. They watched the van for any movement, but could see none. Then, just as they were about to start walking again, Briar saw a flash of light through the driver's window. She nudged the others. There was somebody in there, all right. After the flash died away, a pinprick of orange light swelled and then faded again. Whoever was in the van was smoking a cigarette.

The children retreated, and tried another way. They kept to the quiet roads and alleyways, eventually arriving on the street parallel to theirs. The backyards of these homes met the backyards of those in their own street, separated only by a fence. They moved slowly and cautiously until they could see their home. The rear porch light was on and they could tell that the door was open, but no one could be seen.

Briar was just about to walk towards it when she felt a hand on her arm. Flynn put his finger to his lips and pointed. She strained her eyes, and after a moment she spotted the car parked beneath a large roadside tree, which cast a deep, dark shade under the streetlights. She could just make out the silhouettes of three men inside. They were turning their heads constantly, scanning the street. As quietly as they could, the children retreated to a safe distance.

"We can't get near the house," said Paddy. "What are we going to do now?"

Flynn looked grim. "We have to let our parents know what's happening somehow. They'll be worried."

Paddy suddenly grinned, his teeth flashing in the darkness. "I've got it. Lightning!"

Flynn clapped him on the back. "Good thinking!"

Paddy whistled – a piercing, short blast. It echoed around the silent neighbourhood. The children hunkered down, waiting for the falcon to appear. But after a minute, there was still no sign of the bird. Paddy tried again, louder this time. Again, they waited in silence.

*"Squee!"*

The call was faint and distant, but Briar was in no doubt: it was Lightning! Paddy whistled once more, and Lightning replied, closer this time.

Suddenly the falcon fluttered down out of the night sky, coming in to settle on Paddy's shoulder.

"Hello, boy," said Paddy, stroking the bird's tawny plumage.

"Oh wow. He's beautiful," exclaimed Beth.

"Come and meet him," said Paddy, and Beth stepped forward and raised her hand to stroke Lightning. To her delight the falcon stepped onto it. He seemed immediately at ease with Beth.

"He likes you," said Briar.

"I'll write a note," said Flynn, opening his school bag and ripping some paper from an exercise book. Making use of the light from a street lamp, he began to write.


*Dear Mum and Dad,*

*I'm afraid we're in a bit of trouble. When we left school today we were chased by the police. The Pitbull must be behind it, because he's trying to stop a protest against Dragon World which, as you've probably already guessed, we're a part of.*

*We have to stay out of sight until Saturday – when Dragon World opens – or we'll be arrested.*

Flynn stopped writing and looked at Paddy and Briar. "Should we let them know we're hoping to actually stop Dragon World somehow?"

"Um… perhaps it's best we leave that part out," said Briar. "It'll only worry them more. Just tell them we'll be safe and we'll keep in contact when we can. Tell them I'll deliver myself to The Pitbull on Saturday."

Flynn nodded, and continued writing. When he'd finished, he rolled up the note in a tight scroll and fixed it to Lightning's leg. Lightning had hopped onto Briar's shoulder, so she crept back along the road until she was in sight of the house.

"Wait!"

Briar turned to see Flynn running swiftly up behind her. He whispered urgently.

"I've had a thought. The last time we came to the city, before we met you, we were given a lift by a man named Kelly, and he was really nice.

He'd been surfing at the beach we washed up on, and he bought us something to eat, and drove us into the city. He told us to let him know if we ever needed any help, so maybe he'll let us stay with him for the next two days. We still have his phone number, but it's inside, in Paddy's treasure box. Perhaps Mum and Dad could send Lightning back to us with it."

Briar nodded. She took the note from Lightning's leg and Flynn scribbled his message on the bottom before re-attaching it to the falcon.

"OK." Flynn nodded.

"Home!" Briar commanded, flicking the falcon up into the air. Lightning took off like an arrow, silently speeding through the night in the direction of the house. Briar tried to keep an eye on him, but it was difficult in the darkness.

In seconds Lightning appeared again, picked out by the porch light, and Briar saw him come in to land. Then he began hopping towards the door.

The man came out of the darkness with the speed of a striking snake. He dived across the porch and grabbed Lightning in his outstretched hand.

"Oh no!" Briar gasped, completely forgetting that she was hiding. Flynn grabbed her arm. As they watched, the man backed carefully away from the porch, holding the bird tightly. Briar then watched him inspect the falcon. Lightning made no sound; he didn't even move, and she feared that he'd been hurt, crushed by the oaf's powerful hand! The man spotted the note, and took it from the bird's leg. He unrolled it, and held it up to read it in the dim light.

Lightning chose that moment to rouse himself. He pecked the man's hand so viciously that he yelped loudly and loosened his grip. The guard forgot all about the note, dropping it on the ground. Once the falcon had his wings free he flapped them wildly, buffeting his attacker about the face and scratching at his hands with raking slashes of his talons. The man couldn't help it – he let the bird go. Lightning streaked away, heading back to Flynn and Briar.

Briar watched it all with horror. Lightning could have been killed! Instantly, she made up her mind.

"I'm going to give myself up."

"What!?" said Flynn. "No! You can't! You…"

Briar held up her hand. "Stop, Flynn. I have to go to my uncle anyway. This just means I'm going a little earlier. It will give me more time to find out what I can about Dragon World."

Flynn nodded reluctantly.

"OK," he said. He looked awful, racked with worry.

"I'll try to convince them to let me go inside, and I'll let your parents know you're OK," said Briar. "I've memorised Beth's number. I'll contact you that way – if I can."

Flynn hugged her in the darkness.

"Stay alert, try to notice everything around you," he said. "And be careful."

"I will," she said, trying to muster a smile. "Good luck. I'll see you on Saturday."

She didn't feel half as confident as she sounded, but before she could change her mind she jogged off into the darkness, straight towards the house.

# CHAPTER 16

The Pitbull's phone pealed loudly, startling him. He was lying in a deep bath and dreaming of what he would do to his niece and those brothers when he got his hands on them. He had to admit he'd been surprised when his men had called to let him know that they were involved in the Dragon World protest alongside that pesky schoolgirl. Would they never give up? He smiled to think that their only course of action now was to stand around holding stupid signs, but the smile disappeared when he thought of how easily they'd given the police the slip this afternoon.

Irritably, he dried his hands on a towel and answered the phone.

"What?"

"Er... hello sir, how are you this evening?" It was one of his guards.

"Stop blathering!" ordered The Pitbull.

"Yes s-sir," stammered the guard. "Sir, I have your niece here. The police called us and said she just walked right up to them and introduced herself, and now they've turned her over to me."

The Pitbull sat up, delighted.

"Wonderful. And the rest of them?"

"Who, sir?"

"The two brothers and the other girl, you idiot!" he yelled. "Where are they?"

"Oh, them, sir. Sorry, sir. Your niece says she doesn't know where they are. They've run away, sir."

"Where?"

"I don't know, sir."

The Pitbull threw his champagne glass against the wall, where it shattered into a thousand pieces.

"Tell the police to keep looking for them. We have to find them!"

"Yes, sir. But…"

"But what?" screamed The Pitbull.

"Well… should I bring your niece to you first, sir?"

The Pitbull thought for a moment.

"Yes," he said.

"Erm, sir?"

"What?"

"She says she needs to go into the house to get her clothes and things. Should I let her?"

The Pitbull considered. She'd turned herself in, so she was hardly going to run away again. Plus, it might be fun to give her this little piece of hope, and then do something nasty, like set all her belongings on fire when she arrived.

"Give her five minutes to gather what she needs," he said.

"Yes, sir," said the guard and hung up.

The Pitbull sank back into the bath and smiled. He was going to make Briar's life a misery, and he'd enjoy every minute of it.

# CHAPTER 17

"Where have you been? Where's Briar?"

The question hung in the air, and sounded like an accusation to Flynn. He couldn't bring himself to answer. He'd just let her go. She had been so confident, so assured of her decision, but now she was gone he felt physically sick. She had walked boldly up to the car, and the three policemen waiting there in the shadows hadn't been able to believe their good fortune. They'd simply got out of their car and grabbed her. They'd discussed what to do for a few minutes, and then turned her over to the guard outside the house – the same brute who'd grabbed Lightning. The three policemen had then returned to their car to resume their vigil.

Flynn had watched helplessly as an ugly grin spread across the guard's face, confirming that he was one of The Pitbull's men. He'd gripped Briar roughly by the arm as he pulled out his phone and dialled a number. Flynn couldn't hear what the guard said, but it had been a short call, after which both he and Briar had disappeared inside the house. He'd watched for almost five more minutes, but they didn't come out again so Flynn assumed they'd left via the front door. Reluctantly, he headed down the street, back to Beth and Paddy.

Eventually, he found his voice, and told them what had happened, and all three children sat in stunned silence for a few moments.

"She's so brave," said Beth.

"Sure is," agreed Flynn.

Paddy kicked a stone. "What now?" he said.

Lost for an answer, Flynn closed his eyes in the darkness and tried to think. He almost yelled out loud when suddenly he felt something wet nuzzle his hand.

"Coco!" he exclaimed.

Their beautiful dog stood before them, her tail wagging so hard it made her whole body wriggle.

She made no sound, but leaped up on the children, including Beth, who patted her lovingly.

"She's gorgeous!" she exclaimed.

"And she's brought us a message," said Paddy, who'd seen the rolled-up paper beneath her collar. Flynn grabbed it, hurriedly smoothing it out. It was a tatty envelope. He turned it over.

"I don't believe it," he exclaimed, laughing quietly. "She did it."

There, in his hand, scrawled on the back of the envelope, was their old friend Kelly's number.

"Can I borrow your phone, Beth?" he asked.

# CHAPTER 18

"I wondered if I'd ever see you boys again. I'm glad you called."

Kelly was pouring coffee. He offered it around, and Paddy accepted, but spat the bitter liquid back into his cup as soon as he tasted it.

"What is that?" he cried, making Kelly laugh out loud.

"Sorry. It's an acquired taste," he said. "How about a hot chocolate instead?"

Paddy had never tasted one of those before either, but Beth nodded vigorously and Paddy remembered the taste of the chocolate bar Kelly had given them the day they'd first met. They'd been walking from the beach where they'd washed up after their boat sank, and they were so exhausted they were almost at a standstill. Kelly had spied them on his way to go surfing, and when he returned they were still stumbling along the road. Taking pity on them, he'd stopped to offer his help. The boys were dog-tired, and their clothes were ripped and dirty. He gave them a lift into the city in his old car, and bought a whole bag full of food, most of which they'd never tried before. They'd fallen upon it, not having eaten for a long time. They'd never forgotten his kindness, and he was no different now – making sure they'd all had enough breakfast and slept well.

Last night, when Flynn had called Kelly, he'd been in bed reading a book, but immediately leaped up, got in his car and came to pick up the children, Coco and Lightning. He'd asked no questions, but just accepted that his help was needed, and told them he'd do whatever they asked.

"Can we please stay with you for a couple of nights?" Flynn had asked nervously.

"Is that all?" Kelly replied without hesitation. "Of course!"

They'd driven away from the city, out towards the coast.

"I thought you lived in the city?" said Flynn, confused.

Kelly had smiled. "Remember I told you my dream was to buy a little house by the sea? Well – that dream came true."

The children had tumbled onto mattresses Kelly pulled out of cupboards and laid on the living room floor. They barely had the energy to say goodnight before falling asleep, exhausted. Paddy's last thought had disturbed him, however. He wondered if Briar had a bed to sleep in.

The two brothers, Beth, and Kelly sat in the kitchen now, drinking their hot chocolates and coffee, and admiring Kelly's artwork, which covered every wall of the house. They were great canvases filled with crashing waves and ancient shipwrecks, lighthouses and lonely seabirds. The kitchen looked out over the ocean, and Paddy could see the waves marching towards the beach in ordered, corduroy lines. Coco scampered playfully at their feet along with Kelly's dog – a little fox terrier named Jack. Lightning perched on the kitchen bench, staring intently at each of them as if he was following their conversation.

"Briar would love this house," said Flynn.

Paddy agreed. It reminded him of their home on The Island.

"Who's Briar?" asked Kelly.

The brothers spent all morning filling Kelly in on what had happened since they'd last met. They went for a long walk on the beach, talking all the way. Kelly became more and more agitated as he listened to their story.

"I'll be there to protest on Saturday. I'm going to make the biggest sign you've ever seen in your life!" he declared. They'd arrived home, and they went inside, laughing. Kelly was so positive it made them all feel better.

"In the meantime, how else can I help?" he asked.

Beth picked up her laptop.

"What's your WiFi password?" she asked.

"It's time to hack into Dragon World."

# CHAPTER 19

The Pitbull sat in the control room, waiting impatiently for his niece.

Last night, when Briar arrived, he'd simply ordered that her belongings be incinerated and she herself be locked up in a room on the top floor of the stadium. It was windowless, and completely secure. He had fully intended leaving her there and throwing away the key, but this afternoon, while he'd been practising his opening speech, he suddenly had a wonderful idea. He realised that showing Briar exactly what he had in store for her precious dragons would hurt her terribly. So The Pitbull had decided that a grand tour was in order.

The door opened and in came Briar, shoved along by a guard. She looked pleasingly wretched. He grinned at her and saw her shudder.

He began the tour by showing her around the control room, where all the technical wizardry happened. He didn't understand any of it, but he got a great kick out of the fact that it was all operated by his voice. "Bulb, rise," he'd say, and up it would go. He could open the trapdoors simply by saying the words 'trapdoors, open'. He could start the smoke machine, the lights, the music – everything – with a simple command through the intercom.

His men stood patiently by while he tried it all out for the umpteenth time, clapping his hands with glee. He saw Briar wincing through it all, no doubt imagining the effect that all the lights, smoke, and music would have on the dragons.

Then The Pitbull had a devilish idea. He opened his laptop to check on his bank balance.

There was another zero that hadn't been there yesterday morning – or was it two? He took great pleasure in showing Briar just how much he was profiting from the whole enterprise.

The intercom crackled into life. "Sir, we need to open the garage doors to the cage room. The truck carrying the dragons' food has arrived."

The Pitbull smiled and looked at his watch. Right on time.

"Cage room, open," he commanded. The squeal of the huge steel door opening could be heard through the intercom before the connection was cut. Everything was running like clockwork.

The Pitbull decided he'd continue the tour with a visit to the cage room. When the lift doors opened, he stood back so that Briar could exit first and get the full impact of seeing eighty dragons in captivity.

Her anguished gasp as she entered the room gave him great satisfaction. He looked at her face, and saw that she was trying not to cry, and failing. A tear rolled down her cheek.

Suddenly, Briar ran forward with a desperate cry.

"Iris!"

She fell to her knees beside a cage housing an enormous, bright blue dragon, with wings the colour of sunflowers. It looked like the same one that had tried to attack The Pitbull in the bulb! Reaching through the bars without fear, Briar stroked the creature's nose. The dragon lifted its head, but dropped it back to the floor again almost immediately.

"Iris, you poor sweetheart," she said, sobbing softly. "What have they done to you?"

"How touching," said The Pitbull. "She has names for them." He was delighted – this was just how he'd hoped she'd react.

"Come along," he said. "I have one more thing to show you."

But Briar wouldn't move from the blue dragon's cage. In the end he had to get one of the guards to pry her fingers from the bars and drag her along the floor.

A few cages further along, The Pitbull stopped.

"Drop her," he ordered, then continued to Briar, "I think you might be very interested to see what's in here."

Briar looked up, and when she saw what was in the cage she let out an anguished howl.

"Ahi!"

The baby dragon hopped across the cage floor to Briar, who put her arms through the bars and hugged the creature.

"I'm glad you like him," said The Pitbull.

"She's a her!" snapped Briar.

"Whatever," he replied. "That little beast will be the first dragon the world ever sees. I'm going to put it on a leash, like a dog, and it will accompany me into the bulb. Together we'll rise up to glory."

Suddenly a ferocious roar ripped through the cage room, followed by the sound of a huge body crashing into steel bars. The Pitbull spun around.

Across the room, the green dragon thrashed in its cage and tore at the bars with its talons. It hurled itself against the door again and again.

"Elton!" Briar screamed, and rose to her feet.

"Grab her," instructed The Pitbull, and two guards came forward and gripped her by the arms. She kicked like a mule. "Put a tranquilliser into that dragon," he ordered. A keeper ran over to a rack on the wall where hundreds of tranquilliser darts were lined up alongside a dozen of the guns that fired them.

"So that must be the dragon that belongs to those two little rats?" said The Pitbull. "Thank you for letting me know, Briar. I'll have to make extra-special arrangements for him."

He barked at the guards: "Take her back to the cell."


Back in the control room, the exhausted stadium manager rubbed his eyes. He printed out the checklist of things he still had to do before tomorrow's grand opening and scanned the list before attaching it to his clipboard, satisfied. He took a large bunch of keys from a hook and put them into his pocket. He turned around, scanning the desk in front of him, and a confused look came over his face. Lifting up papers and moving aside trays of documents, he searched the desk thoroughly. But the thing he wanted wasn't there. He turned to the others in the room, all quietly working away, their faces dimly lit by the light from their computer screens.

"Has anyone seen my phone?" he asked.

A couple of them shrugged, but no one said a word.

"Hmmm," he said to himself. "I wonder where I left it?"

# CHAPTER 20

When her phone bleeped, Beth nearly jumped out of her skin. She was concentrating so fiercely on the task at hand, she'd quite forgotten about the world around her. She was shocked to see that the sun had gone down and it was quite dark outside. She'd lost all track of time, having spent the entire afternoon hacking into the Dragon World computer system. The boys had long since left with Kelly, opting to drive around the stadium to see if there was a way in.

She stood up and stretched, sore from sitting for so long. Opening the fridge, Beth poured herself a tall glass of water and drank it in one go.

When she opened the text she almost dropped the phone. She read it several times over, her heart pounding with excitement.

*Beth, it's Briar. I've got a phone – I stole it from one of the men. I have lots to tell you. I can't call you – there's a guard outside my door – but I will text you everything I found out. I'm going to send it to you in short texts, in case I'm discovered. There might be a hidden camera in my cell.*

Beth replied with a simple text: 'Standing by'. She stood in the kitchen, her phone in one hand, the empty glass in the other. For thirty seconds nothing happened. She could barely breathe, and suddenly had an awful thought; if Briar didn't have the phone on silent mode, it would have pinged when Beth's reply text came through, alerting the guard outside. She might have blown it for Briar!

But then, wonderfully, her phone lit up, vibrated and pinged. It pinged a second time, a third, and a fourth. Beth breathed a sigh of relief, and watched as the texts filled the screen. She read them quickly, anxious for information.

One of them gave her an idea. It read:

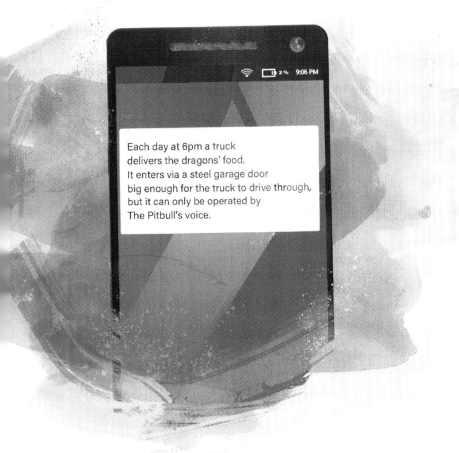

Each day at 6pm a truck
delivers the dragons' food.
It enters via a steel garage door
big enough for the truck to drive through,
but it can only be operated by
The Pitbull's voice.

Beth's fingers shook with excitement as she replied to Briar. But before she could press 'send', a final message came through from Briar. It had no words, but was a simple audio file, a recording. Beth tapped on it and listened, her excitement growing by the second.

Flynn hadn't said a word the whole way home. He knew Kelly was worried about him; he could see his friend looking sideways at him from time to time as he drove. Paddy kept up a constant chatter from the back, trying to figure out how they were going to get into Dragon World.

Paddy always thought out loud, but Flynn needed silence. The stadium was like a fortress – impregnable, with high, smooth walls and heavily guarded at every entrance. They hadn't even been able to get close to it; there was a fence surrounding the entire stadium, with a checkpoint for all vehicles at both the front and back entrances. Half a dozen men stood guard.

Kelly pulled into the driveway and wordlessly Flynn got out of the car. All he wanted to do was sleep, to escape from the constant turmoil in his mind, but he knew he wouldn't fall asleep unless they had a clear plan with some chance of success.

As soon as he opened the front door he saw Beth. She was clearly waiting for them, and barely able to sit still. A broad smile spread across her face.

"I've got a plan," she said.

"Good!" exclaimed Paddy from behind Flynn. "Because Flynn here doesn't have a clue what to do next!"

Flynn couldn't help it; he laughed.

"Neither do you," he said to Paddy.

"Hurry up!" urged Beth. She could barely contain her excitement. "Sit down."

Flynn, Paddy, and Kelly settled into the comfortable chairs. Beth turned her laptop around so they could see the screen.

"Here's what we're going to do," she said, her eyes flashing.

# CHAPTER 21

When Beth finished telling them her plan, Paddy sat back in astonishment. He couldn't believe how brilliant and daring it was, and yet there was so much that could go wrong. It was frightening to even consider carrying it out, much less actually doing it. He looked at his brother. Flynn stared straight ahead, nodding, deep in thought, but a smile played on his lips.

"This could work," he said, more to himself than anyone else.

"Beth, you are one amazing girl," said Kelly, "but it's midnight, and I think the best thing we can do now is go to bed and sleep on it. Tomorrow looks like it's going to be a big day."

Paddy slept like a log for the first time since leaving The Island. Despite not knowing what would happen the next day, he was at peace because at least they were doing something, and not sitting idly by watching their world crumble around them.

In the morning, he was the last to get up. But he could see that Flynn and Beth were well rested, and that they felt the same as he did. They moved with purpose, their strength renewed.

"Morning sleepyhead," said his brother. "What time do you call this?"

"Breakfast time," he replied. "I'm starving. What's on the menu, Kelly?"

Kelly smiled.

"I've got a power smoothie to start with, followed by buckwheat pancakes and maple syrup," he said.

"I have no idea what any of that is," replied Paddy, "but I'll take as much as you've got, thanks. As long as there's no coffee involved!"

"I promise," said Kelly, laughing.

"Paddy, look at this," said Flynn. He pushed a large sheet of paper across the table. "Beth printed it out. It's a plan of the stadium. Look, you can see everything on it; the cage room – where the dragons are kept – the control room, The Pitbull's office, the lobby, everything. In one of Briar's texts last night she said she was in a cell on the seventh floor, right at the top. We reckon it must be one of these rooms, see?" He tapped his finger on the plan.

Paddy nodded. "Can we make another copy, so we can both have one?" he asked. Beth agreed, and clicked away on her laptop.

For the rest of the morning, Beth, Flynn, and Paddy refined their plans. Kelly hovered nearby, making hot chocolate and more food, and offering the occasional suggestion. They briefly stopped for lunch, and then got straight back to work. Paddy watched as Beth negotiated her way doggedly through the Dragon World computer system, cracking passwords and disabling firewalls. She even managed to hack into the stadium manager's emails.

"Look!" she cried, opening one of the email attachments.

The brothers and Kelly gathered around.

"What is it?" asked Flynn.

"It's the schedule for the entire grand opening. It says what's going to happen, at what time."

"Well done!" said Flynn.

The children read it over and over, committing it to memory, and trying to figure out where their opportunities lay.

Finally, Kelly tapped his watch.

"It's five o'clock," he said. "Time to go."

# CHAPTER 22

The dress rehearsal had run without a hitch. There was just the right amount of smoke, the lights looked incredible – even in the daytime – and the thumping rock-and-roll soundtrack was perfect. The dragons behaved themselves wonderfully. He'd told the musical director to add some inspirational, orchestral music just as the bulb was rising out of the ground, and it lent just the right air to the occasion; and to himself, he thought. The Pitbull couldn't wait for the real thing.

"That was wonderful, sir!" exclaimed the stadium manager. "Bravo on your performance."

"Yes. I was rather good, wasn't I?" he agreed.

The Pitbull couldn't believe it; all his dreams and aspirations were about to come true. People would talk about him forever, they'd speak his name with the respect and awe it deserved.

He suddenly felt the need to celebrate. He snapped at one of the guards.

"Go and get the largest bottle of Champagne you can find and put it on ice. Bring it to the cage room at 7pm with plenty of glasses. Make sure all the staff are there on time."

"Yes, sir." The guard hurried away.

The Pitbull spoke to each of his men in turn, grilling them on their preparations. When he was finally satisfied, he left, taking the lift to the seventh floor.

He nodded to the guard, who unlocked the door to Briar's cell. The Pitbull stepped inside to find his niece curled up on the hard floor. She didn't even turn around. She was broken. He'd crushed her spirit. He smiled to himself. He wasn't done with her yet. She had to see the totality of her failure. She had to witness opening night.

"Put on your best dress, my dear," he said, laughing. "You're going to a show."

As The Pitbull made to leave, he snapped an order at the guard.

"Bring her downstairs to the cage room at 7pm. I'm treating everybody to a little opening-night party."

# CHAPTER 23

The streets through the centre of the city were thick with traffic. People hung out of car windows holding Dragon World flags and cheering, letting everyone know they had tickets to opening night. On the way, Kelly had turned on the car radio and every channel was filled with excited announcers babbling about the grand opening. After a while, Flynn couldn't stand it any more and turned it off.

"This had better work," he said under his breath. Beside him, Paddy was unusually silent. Lightning perched on his shoulder. Beth, too, sat quietly.

She stroked Coco's head and stared out of
the window.

"Are you lot ready?" asked Kelly. "Thirty seconds."

Flynn nodded. He turned to the back seat and put
out his hand, palm down. Paddy and Beth put theirs
on top. "Let's go get our dragons – and Briar," he
said grimly.

Kelly took a quick look in the rear-view mirror, and
then hit the brakes.

"Go," he said. "Good luck."

The three children jumped out of the car while it
was still moving and ran hard for the undergrowth
edging the road, keeping as low as possible. Coco
followed silently. The children disappeared into the
brush before the car even passed by. This was a
side road, and traffic was sparse. Paddy launched
Lightning into the air as they went, and the falcon
flew in circles high above them.

Moving quickly and quietly, they set off across
country, pushing through the low trees and scrub,
making their way across empty land towards the

highway that led to the stadium. Twenty minutes later they could see their goal. Flynn checked the watch that Kelly had given him. They had less than half an hour.

When they reached the traffic lights they quickly set to work. Flynn lay at the base of the pole, screwdriver in hand, careful to stay out of sight of passing vehicles. Swiftly he took out the screws from the plate covering the electrical wiring. Meanwhile, Paddy unrolled a length of wire, running it from the base of the traffic lights back into the bushes, where Beth had opened her laptop. She plugged one end of the wire into the computer, then wriggled forward to help Flynn. He moved aside, and watched as Beth pulled out two of the wires from the pole and cut them with pliers. She twisted them around the exposed wires of the cable, and covered the connections with tape. Together, she and Flynn slid backwards into the cover of the undergrowth.

"Let's give it a try," said Beth, clicking rapidly on the touchpad of her laptop.

She looked down the road. A vanload of people were heading towards them, bound for Dragon World. She clicked on the touchpad. The traffic lights turned red instantly, and the van came to a halt. They could hear the excited voices of the people inside. She clicked again, the light turned green, and the van continued on its way.

"Bingo," said Paddy. "Nice work, Beth."

"Thanks," she replied. "Now you two get in position. Good luck!"

Flynn and Paddy crept forward again, and lay down in the bushes at the edge of the highway. Paddy whistled for Lightning, and the bird fluttered down and settled beside them.

Flynn looked at Paddy.

"Are you scared?"

"Scared stiff," replied Paddy, smiling.

"Me too," said Flynn. "Oh – here we go. Look."

A truck rumbled along the highway towards them. As it came closer, Flynn could see the driver and another man in the passenger seat.

"Got it?" he called to Beth over his shoulder.

"Got it," came her reply. "Stand by."

Flynn saw the traffic lights turn red and to his relief he heard the truck slow down. He got ready to run.

Paddy suddenly spoke.

"How do we know it's the right truck?" he asked.

Flynn looked at his watch. 5.50pm.

"We don't," he replied.

"I thought you might say that," said Paddy.

The truck rumbled to a halt.

Paddy whistled – three short bursts – and Lightning rose into the air, flapping hard. He flew around to the front of the truck and hovered there, staring at the two men through the windscreen. They stared back in surprise.

Paddy whistled once more, as softly as he could, and Lightning swooped. Talons first, he smashed into the windscreen so hard a crack shot up it, snaking its way from top to bottom.

"Go!" hissed Flynn, and he and Paddy bolted for the truck. Together they skidded underneath it, lay on their backs and searched desperately for something to hold on to. There was an array of pipes to grab, but the first one Flynn touched was burning hot and he recoiled. Beside him, Paddy hauled himself up into a space on one side of the engine, and he gestured wildly at Flynn to get into the other side.

Suddenly, the truck began to move, lurching forward. Flynn scrambled backwards, his feet rapidly working at the ground to get purchase. He gripped the pipe and, ignoring the pain searing up his arm from the scorching metal, pulled himself forward along the belly of the truck until he could grip another one. Thankfully, it was cool to the touch and he held on with both hands. He reached blindly over his head, found a hole in the steel in the engine bay and dragged himself up into the space.

The truck gathered speed along the highway until the road was flashing by beneath them. Flynn's burnt hand was intensely painful, but he closed his eyes and tried to ignore it.

Back in the undergrowth, Beth unplugged the cable, rolled it up and stuffed it in her backpack. She closed her laptop and jammed it in too. She scratched behind Coco's ears, and looked around for Lightning, meaning to congratulate him for distracting the men in the truck. But he was nowhere to be seen. She whistled, and waited. No Lightning. Then, staying low, she set off at a jog towards the stadium.

# CHAPTER 24

**B**riar bashed the phone battery against the concrete floor as quietly as she could, but it still made far too much noise. The guard outside would certainly hear her if she tried any harder.

The phone had died just as she'd been about to send a text to Beth to find out if the boys had been successful in getting on the truck. She hadn't seen that the battery was low, and she cursed herself for not noticing.

She'd read somewhere that you could get a bit more life out of a battery if you dented it, but she knew that if she pierced it, that could be dangerous.

She pushed it against the hinges of the door.

It made a decent dent in the case, but would it

make any difference?

Briar inserted the battery back into the phone

and started it up. To her great relief the screen lit up,

and the battery indicator showed she had three per

cent left. Would it last long enough?

She fired off a quick text to Beth.

*Battery low. Switching off phone now to save it.*
*Will make sure to switch it back on for 6.30pm as*
*you instructed.*

When she looked at the top corner of the screen,

she gave a little cry. The battery was at two per cent.

She took note of the exact time and then powered

it off as quickly as she could. This was going to be

tight. She closed her eyes, took a deep breath and

began to count.

# CHAPTER 25

"Evening, lads. All set for the big night?"

"Wouldn't have a clue, mate. The boss doesn't let us inside."

"Haha – I wouldn't let you lot inside either. You'd only mess up the carpet."

The guards at the checkpoint laughed at the truck driver's joke. Paddy willed them to hurry up – he was almost at his limit. He and Flynn had been hanging upside down from the belly of the truck for over five minutes, and his arms were burning with the effort. He sagged lower and lower with each passing moment, knowing that sooner or later he'd have to let go. He could see Flynn was in a similar state, his eyes closed and his muscles trembling as he struggled to hang on.

Suddenly, Paddy heard the sound of footsteps very close. A guard was walking around the truck! He stopped every now and again to inspect something, and he halted right beside Paddy. Only his legs were visible, and now his knees bent as he began to squat down. He would see the brothers for sure! Paddy made a supreme effort to pull himself back up towards the engine bay without grunting.

At the same time, the driver spoke.

"Come on, lads. Let us through. You don't want us to be late today of all days, do you?"

To Paddy's enormous relief the guard stood up again, and quickly finished his lap of the truck. He banged hard on the tailgate.

"Good to go!" he shouted, and Paddy heard the squeak of the barrier arm rising. The engine revved and they were away again.

"Hold on," he told himself. "Just another minute."

Mercifully the driver sped the short distance to the stadium, no doubt anxious he'd be late and have to face the consequences of an angry Pitbull. He screeched to a halt, and spoke into an intercom mounted on a pole.

"Dragon food delivery," he said.

It seemed an age before Paddy finally heard the harsh screech of the garage door as it rose up. He was done; one hand slipped off the bar and he almost fell right there. Somehow he managed to grip on with his other hand, but only for just long enough for the truck to roll inside the building.

"Flynn," he croaked, and saw his brother glance at him, pain etched into his face. Powerless to do anything else, Paddy let go and landed heavily on his back on the floor. From the corner of his eye he saw Flynn drop too. They had milliseconds to react. He rolled hard to the left, trying to get directly under the centre of the truck so he wouldn't be run over by its huge tyres. He banged into Flynn, trying to do the same thing.

Suddenly, they could see the ceiling as the truck moved on. Behind them, the steel door shrieked as it began to descend.

Paddy thought he saw something in his peripheral vision – a small projectile speeding silently through the air.

"Get up!" urged Flynn, and the brothers rolled into a crouch. There was a foot-wide gap between the wall and a large cage and they made for it, not stopping to look whether anyone was watching.

They dived into the space, Paddy landing heavily on his brother's legs. There they lay, not daring to move or speak. Suddenly, Lightning swooped down and landed on top of Paddy. The falcon perched there staring at them, clearly displeased to have been abandoned.

"You silly bird!" Paddy hissed. "What are you doing here?" Lightning, as if to reply, dug his talons into Paddy's skin. Paddy grinned and grimaced at the same time.

The boys lay silent until they were sure they hadn't been spotted. Flynn finally moved.

"Get off me," he whispered.

They wriggled and twisted in the small space until they could sit up. Just inches away were the silky black scales of an adolescent dragon. It lay on the bottom of its cage, curled up in a ball. It must have known they were there beside it, thought Paddy, but it didn't move at all – even to look at them. Paddy couldn't help himself. He reached in and stroked it.

"Don't worry," he whispered. "We're going to get you out."

"Paddy, look," said Flynn with horror.

They could see clear to the other end of the room. Cage after cage was filled with dragons of every colour, shape, and size. And every single one of them lay still, just as the black dragon was doing. Paddy was filled with anger.

"We have to make this work. We have to free them," he insisted.

"Calm down, little brother. We will," replied Flynn, but Paddy could see his brother's jaw clenching, his eyes hard. He felt the same way.

A forklift was working to unload the truck – boxes of fresh meat loaded onto pallets. Men slit open the boxes and pulled out great chunks. They heaved them inside the dragons' cages, but the dragons didn't move or even look at the meat. They all looked skinny, and Paddy wondered if they were eating anything at all.

The brothers ducked down as a guard came along with meat for the black dragon, but he simply threw it in between the bars and walked away. They were safe – for now.

Paddy heard Flynn breathe in sharply, and he turned to see him cradling his hand. Flynn told him he'd burned it on the truck engine. He was clearly in terrible pain.

Paddy tore a strip from the bottom of his shirt. It gave him a pang of pleasure to destroy his uncomfortable school uniform. He wrapped Flynn's hand tightly, trying to ignore the bright pink flesh. Flynn winced, but said nothing. Paddy made him drink some water. Stuffing the bottle back into his backpack, he unzipped the front pocket and took out a handful of nuts and bolts.

"OK?" Paddy asked hopefully.

Flynn nodded. "Thanks."

"Off you go then. I'll count to sixty. Good luck."

Flynn rose and made his way along the wall. Emerging from behind the cage, he worked his way silently up the room towards the far end and the door that was marked on Beth's stadium plan. Paddy saw Flynn slip like a shadow between the last two cages.

"Fifty-seven, fifty-eight, fifty-nine, sixty," counted Paddy. He stood up, and with all his might, threw the nuts and bolts at the far side of the room. They bounced off the walls and clanked off the steel cages.

The men at work near the truck turned around quickly. Two of them walked along between the cages to see what had caused the clatter.

Before Paddy bobbed down out of sight, he saw Flynn open the door and slip through, closing it quietly behind him.

# CHAPTER 26

Beth was thankful that it was almost dark as she worked her way around the stadium perimeter fence. She had seen three guards patrolling out here already – no doubt looking for people trying to get into Dragon World without a ticket.

There was a huge crowd at the main entrance, stretching for half a mile back down the road, and with a thrill Beth realised that some of them were protesters. They held placards and banners and chanted slogans.

She got as close as she dared to the entrance, then found a dense patch of scrub to hide in. She lay down and opened her laptop. From her bag she produced a piece of black cloth Kelly had given her, which she dropped over the computer so passers-by wouldn't see the light from the screen.

Coco lay down quietly beside her.

Then Beth pulled out her phone. She dialled a number, but didn't call it yet. She sat and waited, watching the time count down.

# CHAPTER 27

Flynn's hand throbbed so badly that he was having trouble concentrating on where he was going. He'd managed to get into the service area of the stadium and was walking down a corridor looking for the lift. Distracted, he turned a corner without checking, and almost bumped into two guards. Luckily, they were deep in conversation and didn't notice him.

Backpedalling rapidly, Flynn looked around desperately for somewhere to hide. He tried a door handle and thankfully it opened and he ducked inside, closing the door behind him. The room turned out to be a small kitchen, and he remembered from the stadium plan that there was one on each floor. Flynn stood with his back to the door until the sound of the guards' voices faded away down the hallway. He was just about to open the door again when he noticed on top of some cupboards a plastic container emblazoned with a red cross. He'd read books about the war, and knew that the cross was a sign for medical supplies.

Glancing at his watch, Flynn pulled the kit down and opened it, knowing he'd have to hurry. He turned it upside down on the bench, spreading out the contents. He spotted a tube with a label that said Burn Salve. Unwrapping the bandage from his hand, Flynn squeezed the salve onto his fiery red skin and immediately felt relief as the numbing coolness did its work. He rewrapped the bandage, opened the door and sneaked out into the hallway.

The lift was only twenty yards further down the hall. There was no one to be seen, so he stood nervously in the open, waiting for it to arrive. It took just a few seconds. He stepped in, and pressed the button for the seventh floor. As the lift began to move, Flynn pulled the stadium plan out of his pocket and studied it.

If they were correct, and Briar was in the cell at the end of the hallway, he'd have to be careful when the lift door opened. The guard outside Briar's door would have a clear view down the hallway.

*Ping!* The lift came to a stop and the doors opened. Flynn didn't get out, but waited and listened. As the doors began to close again he reached out his hand to stop them, holding it over the sensor to keep them open just as Kelly had taught him. With his other hand he took a small mirror and a coil of rope from his backpack.

Holding the mirror by the lift door at just the right angle, Flynn was able to see a reflection of the hallway. Sure enough, the guard was there, and he was alert. He must have heard the ping of the lift. To Flynn's horror, the guard rose from his chair and began to walk down the hallway towards him.

Flynn checked his watch.

## CHAPTER 28

"Fifty-seven, fifty-eight, fifty-nine, sixty." Briar took a deep breath, and pushed the power button on the phone. For an awful moment, she thought the phone was dead, but it flickered and glowed and the maker's logo appeared on the screen.

A few seconds later it booted itself up and she gasped: the battery was at one per cent! The time display showed 6:29pm. As quickly as she could, she navigated to the phone's settings and set the ring volume as loud as it would go.

Briar heard the guard's footsteps out in the hallway, but they seemed to be moving in the wrong direction; he was walking away from her cell! She stared at the phone in desperation.

Outside in the darkness, hiding in the bushes just back from the Dragon World perimeter fence, Beth pressed the 'dial' button on her phone.

# CHAPTER 29

The guard had almost reached the lift when Flynn heard the phone ring in Briar's cell. It resounded clearly in the silence but rang for no more than a few seconds before the noise distorted and slowed and finally faded away with an electronic squeak.

"What the…?" exclaimed the guard in the hallway. He turned on his heel and sprinted for Briar's cell.

Flynn didn't hesitate. Grabbing his rope, he emerged from the lift into the hallway, his heart pounding in his chest. He ran as lightly as he could, his footfalls drowned out by the heavy clomping of the guard's boots. He was no more than ten feet behind the man, and closing fast.

The guard had no idea that Flynn was chasing him. He fumbled for the key hanging from his belt as he ran, and had it in his hand by the time he reached the door to the cell. Jamming it into the lock and turning it, he slammed his bulk into the door to fling it open. He bellowed at Briar.

"Where's the phone?! I heard it ring!"

The short time the guard hesitated at the door was all it took for Flynn to catch him up. As the guard strode into the cell Flynn threw himself into the man's back at a full sprint, and the two of them catapulted across the room. They slid across the cell floor together, crashing into the far wall. The guard's head struck the concrete with a sickening crunch, and he groaned in pain.

Flynn wasted no time uncoiling his rope and hauling the guard's hands up behind his back. He quickly began tying loops around the man's wrists, but he struggled, and Flynn yelled for Briar to help. She promptly sat down hard on the guard's legs.

Flynn almost had him trussed up, but the guard was strong, and he bucked wildly, throwing the two children off his back. He then rose to his knees, and Flynn had to let go. The rope was rapidly uncoiling from the guard's wrists.

"Run!" Flynn yelled to Briar, and they took off together. Flynn slammed the cell door behind them, and was relieved to see the key was still in the lock. He turned it just in time before the door shuddered under the tremendous impact of the guard throwing himself against it. He roared like a wild animal as Flynn and Briar bolted back down the hallway to the waiting lift.

# CHAPTER 30

The guards had all left the cage room. They'd even abandoned the little office. Paddy and Lightning were quite alone with the dragons, and Paddy was at Elton's cage. The sight of his beautiful dragon imprisoned like this almost broke his heart. Paddy hauled on the lock as hard as he could, but he knew it was useless. He might as well be trying to break into a bank vault. It was solid steel, with a bolt thicker than his thumb.

Elton put his great head to the bars, and Paddy reached in and stroked him, desperate with frustration.

This had to work; they must free the dragons!

A tear rolled down Paddy's cheek; he could see how lost Elton was, how sad at being separated from Iris and Ahi. The floor of Elton's cage was littered with empty tranquilliser darts; they'd been using them on the great dragon to keep him docile. There was a long rack of them on the wall, each one a glass tube of glowing blue liquid, topped with an evil spike.

Blinking away his tears, Paddy ran to greet Iris, and finally Ahi. The baby dragon snickered gently inside the cage, and nuzzled Lightning, who'd hopped through the bars to greet her.

Pulling himself together, Paddy left Lightning in the cage with Ahi and took a walk around the vast room, taking care to stay out of sight of the security cameras.

"Don't give up," he whispered to himself, over and over. "Think."

Along each wall, spaced about ten feet apart, short, wide tubes protruded about six inches. As Paddy wondered what they could be for, he gradually became aware of a rumble, a deep vibration that hummed through the building. It built and built, and suddenly he realised what it was: one hundred and fifty thousand people entering the stadium and taking their seats for the show! A pulse of anger rippled through him.

Suddenly, the lift pinged and its doors slid open. Paddy dived for cover. Two men emerged, each pushing a stainless steel trolley. On the first was an ice bucket containing the biggest bottle Paddy had ever seen. On the second two dozen glasses rattled and clinked. The men arranged the trolleys in the middle of the cage room.

"French Champagne," one said, examining the bottle. "This'll be nice."

"I still can't believe it," the other replied, shaking his head.

They got back into the lift.

As Paddy stared at the giant bottle of Champagne, a fiendish idea popped into his mind!

# CHAPTER 31

"They'll find out I've escaped," puffed Briar. "My uncle is expecting me in the cage room at 7pm. He told the guard to bring me there. They're having some sort of opening night celebration for the staff."

"Oh great," replied Flynn, glancing at his watch. They had less than five minutes before the alarm was raised. They were halfway back to the cage room, taking the stairs instead of the lift. Guards were everywhere, making last-minute preparations. This wasn't part of the plan, that was for sure.

He hadn't counted on the entire staff of Dragon World being in the very place they were hoping to escape from.

Even from here, deep in the building, Flynn could hear the huge crowd outside in the arena. They'd started up a chant, and the whole stadium trembled from the vibrations of their stamping feet.

Flynn and Briar flew down the stairs, taking them two at a time. Reaching the bottom of the stairwell, they burst out into the corridor. Thankfully it was empty, and they sprinted along it.

"Wait! Come back," hissed Briar. Flynn turned around, skidding to a halt. He'd run right past the door to the final stairwell leading to the basement and the cage room. Shaking his head, he ran back to Briar.

"What would you do without me, huh?" she asked, smiling.

They bolted down the last flight of stairs. Through the glass panel in the door to the cage room, Flynn saw with relief that they'd made it in time. There were no guards to be seen – yet. He pushed it, and it made a curious squelch as it opened. He noticed the thick rubber seals all around it and briefly wondered what they were for.

"What took you so long?" said Paddy, smiling as he walked towards them.

Flynn was just about to answer when the lift pinged. The three children sprinted madly across the room, diving behind Elton's cage just as the doors opened and a dozen guards emerged.

# CHAPTER 32

"**G**et away from me!"

The Pitbull stood up abruptly and ripped the cape from his neck. Enough was enough. The only reason he'd agreed to wear makeup for the grand opening was because he looked so good in the advertisement. But the way they fussed around him drove him crazy. The makeup artist scuttled away like a cockroach exposed to the light.

Striding from the room, The Pitbull felt like a god. All-powerful. Whatever he wanted, whatever he dreamed of, came to pass. This was it; his night, and his alone! His men were mere minions, there only to do his bidding. In truth, he could probably have done it all without their help. In fact, he was sure of it.

When the lift to the cage room opened, he expected his staff to be standing, perhaps in an expectant semi-circle, ready to explode into rapturous cheering. Instead, they stood about in groups like a bunch of schoolboys, talking amongst themselves. Two of them appeared to be playing a game of rock, paper, scissors!

"Ahem," he coughed.

His men turned, and stared dumbly at him. No one said a word.

The Pitbull swallowed his irritation. Nothing would spoil this night. Nothing!

He grabbed the huge magnum of Champagne, and went to grip the cork, but to his surprise it had already been pulled out.

"Which one of you idiots opened this?" he asked. He had wanted to shake the bottle and spray it around the room in celebration. He was met with only blank stares from his men.

The Pitbull sighed, deciding in that moment that he'd fire all of them once Dragon World was up and running.

"Pour the glasses," he barked to one of the guards, thrusting the bottle into his hands. The man hurriedly obeyed, splashing the foaming liquid liberally into each glass.

The Pitbull picked up his glass. His enthusiasm for this little ceremony had waned.

"A toast," he said, more to himself than anyone else. His staff all raised their drinks.

The Pitbull paused, his glass halfway to his lips, and looked around the room.

"Where's my niece? I ordered her to be brought here."

His stupid men gave him no answer.

"Can you hear me?" he screamed. "I said, WHERE'S BRIAR!?"

The stadium manager stepped forward.

"I don't know, sir. I'll send someone for her immediately."

He nodded at one of the guards, who promptly upended his glass of Champagne, gulping it down in one go before running from the room.

The Pitbull hesitated.

"You know what?" he said. "Forget her. Let's start the show." His miserable niece could wait. He could have her down here suffering every night for the rest of her life if he so chose.

The men cheered, finally, lifting their glasses before draining them thirstily.

"Right, then," said The Pitbull. "Cage 3B, open!"

The bolt on the baby dragon's cage slid back smoothly, and the door sprang open. A broad smile crossed The Pitbull's face. What had Briar called it? Ali? Or Amy, was it? Who cared?

"Get it out," he ordered.

Three men ran into the cage and grabbed the small orange dragon, dragging it across the floor to The Pitbull. It struggled and pushed the three men about somewhat, and he briefly wondered if what he was doing was wise. But the baby dragon seemed to tire quickly, and soon stopped struggling.

"Bring me the collar and lead," he commanded.

One of his men ran forward with it. The Pitbull smiled. The lead had a brass handle, into which was inscribed 'The Dragon Master'. That was him!

He took the collar and went to slip it over the dragon's head. The creature had become quite docile. But just as he made to pass the collar over its snout, he heard a squawk – like a bird – from high up in the rafters. As he looked up to see what had made the noise, the little brute before him nipped his hand! The dragon then gave a mighty struggle, slipping from the men's grasp, and raised its wings. Flapping hard, the creature rose, flying drunkenly from side to side, but gaining height in the process.

His men shouted in surprise, and made to grab the beast, but it rose out of reach, and when it reached the roof it clung onto a rafter and hung upside down.

It was only then that The Pitbull saw the falcon.

"Get that bird!" he screamed to his men. "Shoot it! And the dragon – shoot them both!"

An awful thought flashed through his mind – hadn't his men told him that those brothers had a pet falcon? But no, that was impossible. It was just a coincidence – the bird must have flown in by accident when the garage doors had opened.

He watched grimly as his men wrenched all the tranquilliser guns from the wall and stuffed them with darts.

# CHAPTER 33

**B**eth had held her breath for so long she thought she might burst. Her heart thumped in her chest, and her throat tightened in fear.

The policeman was almost on top of her. She'd watched him coming ever closer as he walked backwards and forwards through the scrub, trying to flush out people hiding in the undergrowth. After everyone attending the show had gone into the stadium, the police had arrived to arrest the protesters and they'd scattered, hiding where they could.

This man was trying to round up the last of them.

Beth could see no good options. If she bolted, she'd have to leave her laptop – trying to run with it in her hands would be impossible and she'd surely be caught. But if she abandoned it they would be lost, and her friends captured.

Coco provided the solution. Emerging from the bushes like a tiger ambushing its prey, she leaped at the man with a ferocious snarl, snapping her jaws rapidly, her teeth flashing in the glare from the stadium lights.

He squealed, then turned and ran for his life. He didn't stop until he'd reached the safety of the road and the other policemen. She saw him talking to them, shaking his head vigorously. He must have been too ashamed to tell them he'd just run away from a dog.

Relieved, Beth scratched Coco behind the ears, and then went back under the cloth to look at her laptop. It was almost time.

It was then that she heard the helicopters. A faint buzz grew to a deafening roar. Beth had been expecting them, but that didn't make them any less frightening. Suddenly the sky was full of them, gigantic black beasts chopping at the air with their dual rotor blades. Coco whined, and shrank against Beth in the darkness.

The choppers roared over Beth's head and rose to hover over the top of the stadium. The crowd would be able to see them through the bars crisscrossing the stadium roof. They flew an intricate pattern of passes over the stadium in an elaborately choreographed routine, before coming together in a spinning tornado of machines, and then flying away to the east. A great roar rose from the crowd. The show had begun.

# CHAPTER 34

The men fired a number of shots at Ahi and Lightning but missed every time. The little dragon and the falcon seemed to be working together, the bird flying from one rafter to another, and then, *squee*, calling for Ahi to follow.

Briar had had to stop herself from running out into the middle of the room several times, and Flynn had stopped her twice. She was beside herself, desperate for Ahi to escape, knowing the men would eventually find their aim. It was only a matter of time.

The Pitbull stood in the middle of the floor, collar and lead in hand, staring up at the dragon and screaming at his men.

None of them, including Briar, noticed Elton and Iris rising up in their cages. No one heard them yipping and snickering to each other.

But everyone noticed the blinding, white-hot rivers of fire that simultaneously spewed from their gaping mouths. Briar and the brothers, hiding amongst the cages, shrank away from the fierce heat. The dragonfire filled the room, crossing the space and rebounding from the walls. It seemed never-ending, a continuous molten gush. Guards screamed in panic and ran for their lives. They were blown clean back along the room before the rolling flames, slapping at their clothes, and bolting through the door. The Pitbull was the last to leave. He screamed with frustration and threw the lead on the ground.

"I'll show you! You'll be sorry!" he bellowed at the dragons. Then he turned and stepped through the doors into the bulb.

# CHAPTER 35

Beth counted down the seconds on her laptop. She doubled checked on her phone. It was time. She took a deep breath.

"Please let this work," she whispered.

She clicked through various windows on her screen. Opening the control panel, she turned on the computer's microphone, putting it on its most sensitive setting. Next, she took her phone and located the audio file that Briar had sent her. She pressed play.

The recording was perfect. The Pitbull's voice came out crystal clear.

"Cage room, open."

Beth stared at her computer screen intently. The voice recognition software in the Dragon World computer system instantly processed the recording and a pop-up appeared on her screen: 'Cage room door is opening."

In the darkness Beth punched the air.

# CHAPTER 36

The Pitbull had been gone no more than thirty seconds, and Flynn, Paddy and Briar had only just emerged from their hiding places when they heard the screech of the steel door lifting up.

"Yes!" exclaimed Paddy. "Beth did it!"

"And perfect timing," agreed Flynn. He couldn't believe they'd got this far. They stood in wonder, watching the door rise up, and felt the cool night air rushing into the room.

"What now?" asked Briar.

"We wait for The Pitbull to open the dragons'

cages, and then we walk right out," said Paddy triumphantly.

"Be careful," warned Flynn. "Stay alert. Keep out of sight of the security cameras. I'm going to say hello to Iris."

Flynn walked over to Iris's cage. She was snickering to Ahi, who'd flown back down and was whimpering and nuzzling her mother through the bars.

"You clever girls," said Flynn. "And when did you learn to fly, Ahi?"

In the silence, Flynn heard the sound of orchestral music thundering around the stadium. He wanted to spoil The Pitbull's show more than anything in the world.

And then he heard another sound, one that chilled him to the bone; the whine of the electric motor that powered the garage door.

"FLYNN!" screamed Paddy. "The door's going to close again!"

Flynn watched as his brother leapt up on one side of the door, climbing the vertical steel supports hand over hand to reach the motor at the top. He hauled on the cover, but it was bolted firmly into place. The door began to move.

"No!" he yelled.

Suddenly, Flynn had an idea. He ran to the guardroom, and there, hanging on a hook, was a set of keys. He hoped they were the right ones.

He leaped into the seat of the forklift and almost slid straight out the other side, he was going so fast. He jammed a key into the ignition and mercifully it shot home. When he turned it the forklift roared into life.

Flynn had no idea how to drive a forklift, but he'd watched Kelly driving his car and hoped the same principles applied.

Stamping on the accelerator, he pulled back on every lever he could see, guessing that one of them would put the machine into reverse. The forklift shot backwards with a squeal of tyres, and Flynn spun the steering wheel to turn it around. He didn't even take his foot off the accelerator as he jammed all the levers forward and the forklift jerked away.

He had little time to figure out how to operate the forks, and as he raced along the floor of the cage room he experimented with the levers. The first one he tried took the machine out of gear, and it slowed. He jammed the lever forward again and kept going. The next one tilted the whole fork mechanism backwards and forwards.

"Come on!" he shouted in frustration.

*CLANG!* The forks glanced off one of the dragons' cages, sending a jarring vibration through the machine, and Flynn cursed himself for not watching where he was going.

"Hurry, Flynn!" screamed his brother, but Flynn didn't dare look up. Another lever seemed to do nothing at all. Finally, he found it. The forks began to rise and he allowed himself to look up. The door was two thirds closed, and was coming down fast! He raised the forks as he raced the last twenty feet, but then saw he'd have to lower them again to get them under the door. He adjusted again and again as he closed the gap.

Flynn was concentrating so hard on getting the fork height correct he realised too late that he hadn't yet figured out where the brakes were. He hit the door at full speed, smashing into it so hard it made his teeth rattle and his ears ring with the noise. The door continued to close, and when it hit the forks the whine of the electric motor rose to a screech. It laboured for a few seconds, then shut itself down.

"Try to open it back up," said Paddy, and Flynn pulled on the lever. The forklift roared and juddered.

The door held fast.

"The dragons won't fit under that," said Briar. "We can barely fit through." There was a gap of no more than twelve inches between the bottom of the door and the ground.

"There's a message on the screen," said Paddy, still hanging off the electric motor. He squinted at it. "It says: 'Malfunction. To reset, enter code 89302 into the security system'. Briar – we need to get this code to Beth!"

Briar shook her head sadly. "I can't. The phone's dead."

# CHAPTER 37

The sight of 150,000 people in a state of rapturous anticipation was nothing short of breathtaking. As The Pitbull had hoped, the helicopters had whipped the crowd into a frenzy. They were ready for him.

When the bulb rose out of the arena floor they spontaneously began performing a Mexican wave, which travelled rapidly, mesmerisingly, around the stadium; a tidal surge of arms rising and falling. They threw everything they were holding in their hands into the air: hats, drinks, children. They screamed their appreciation, almost drowning out the orchestral music.

The Pitbull felt a little strange – a bit light-headed – but he shook it off. It was probably just nerves. Taking a deep breath, he cleared his throat. He pushed the blue button to turn on his microphone. He spread his arms wide.

"WELCOME TO DRAGON WORLD!" he bellowed, his voice booming around the stadium at astonishing volume. A roar rose from the crowd in response, even louder than before.

The Pitbull pressed the intercom.

"Smoke, on," he commanded, and the dry ice cannons immediately began to pour out thick streams.

"Spotlight, on," he said, and a white beam cut across the stadium, lighting up the bulb like a dewdrop in the morning sun.

"Trapdoors, open," he commanded, and he heard the crowd gasp as the trapdoors flew back to reveal a gaping black hole in the centre of the arena.

He switched his microphone back on.

"And now," he said to the crowd, pausing for dramatic effect. "The moment you've all been waiting for. From the far reaches of the Earth, from the dark places, the places where no man – save I – have dared to tread, you're about to see the most fearsome creatures in all existence. Keep your eyes on that awful black pit, ladies and gentlemen. But do not be afraid, for I am here – your protector, your Dragon Master!"

The Pitbull paused again, looking around, drinking in the moment. The crowd had fallen silent – you could have heard a pin drop in the stadium.

"Beyold!" he cried. "I mean, bewold!
I mean, behold!"

The Pitbull shook his head. What was wrong with him? It felt as though the dry ice fog was invading his brain.

The music rose to a stirring crescendo.

"Here, in all their glory, are the beasts of the underworld!" thundered The Pitbull.

He pressed the button on the intercom.

"Cages, open. Hoses, on," he commanded.

All eyes were glued to the black hole at the centre of the arena. Suddenly, a tiny winged creature rose out of it, travelling at a scarcely believable speed. The Pitbull rubbed his eyes and shook his head in disbelief. It was the bird – the falcon! It tore vertically upwards and sped between the bars crisscrossing the roof. In seconds it was lost in the night sky.

The audience erupted with laughter. Then, they all stared at the hole in the middle of the arena, but not a single dragon rose up from it.

The Pitbull's head swam as the seconds ticked by. He felt his legs go weak. He wasn't in full control of them. But a thought crystallised in his mind, and suddenly he was sure. The brothers were here, somehow, down there in the cage room, and they were preventing the dragons from emerging into the arena. His mind twisted like a clenching fist, and focused on just one thing: getting those boys.

"Bulb, down," he croaked.

His tongue felt thick and strange in his mouth as he began to descend.

# CHAPTER 38

When Flynn heard the metallic clank of every bolt on every lock in the cage room shoot back, and saw the doors swing open, he stood, stunned, the awful realisation striking him: the dragons were now free from their cages, but unable to leave their prison.

Only Elton and Iris had emerged, rushing out to greet the children and Ahi. The rest of the dragons remained where they were, curled up on the floor of their cages.

Then Flynn heard a strange sound, like wind rushing through a tunnel. Suddenly, from the hose nozzles all around the cage room, water gushed out with so much force that Flynn, Paddy, and Briar were knocked off their feet. Instantly the floor was swamped, and now the water was rising and filling the room. It poured out through the gap under the garage door, but not nearly quickly enough to negate the speed of the rising water.

"Flynn! Look out!" screamed Briar.

Flynn spun around.

An enormous, ruby-red dragon had heaved itself out of one of the cages at the far side of the room, spurred into action by the gushing water which had been aimed squarely at it. Peering through the flying spray, Flynn suddenly realised that this was Big Red, the dragon he'd been forced to ride back on The Island. The pure, cold fear he'd felt then returned to him now. But Flynn could see the confusion in Big Red's eyes, and immediately felt sorry for him. He waded through the waist-deep water towards him without hesitation, hoping that the dragon would remember that he'd saved his life. The creature towered over the boy, almost reaching the ceiling. Flynn held out his hand, and as they came together the dragon lowered his head. Flynn boldly placed his hand on the dragon's nose. Big Red halted, and looked at Flynn, who saw recognition but also terror in the creature's eyes.

"It's OK," Flynn said, trying to keep his voice calm. "We'll help you."

But the water was rising fast, and the dragon was panicking. He started forward again, and Flynn had to get out of the way quickly. Big Red was making for the trapdoors!

Suddenly, all the dragons were on the move. One by one they emerged from their cages. The nozzles were now under water, and soon the children would have to swim. They were surrounded by dragons on every side, all slashing wildly at the water with their talons and roaring in panic. They knew where to go. Every last dragon was making for the trapdoor – and the arena. Flynn realised that The Pitbull must have rehearsed this many times, teaching the dragons that leaving the cage room and flying out into the arena was their only way of escaping the water.

As Big Red lumbered past Flynn, he reached out and grabbed the leading edge of one of his wings. Hauling himself up onto it, he clambered from there to the dragon's back, then moved forward to sit astride his neck. Looking across at Paddy and Briar, he saw they'd done the same – both were mounted on Elton. Iris had gathered Ahi in her talons, and lifted her clear of the water.

The water filled the room at a tremendous rate. It was now covering the backs of the smaller dragons. They'd be swimming soon.

Grabbing Big Red's spines, Flynn urged him forward, but the creature was already wading through the water as fast as he could.

It took all Flynn's willpower to do what he did next.

"Block the exit! Don't let any of them out!" he cried to Paddy.

Paddy reacted immediately, guiding Elton to the opening. The dragon leaped clear of the water, and clung onto the rafters beside it. Flynn and Big Red arrived seconds later.

Big Red was so tall that his head almost reached the opening. Flynn hauled on his spines. Surely his instinct must have been to escape out into the arena but instead, incredibly, he responded, turning back to face the rest of the oncoming dragons.

# CHAPTER 39

"*Squee!*"

Beth looked up, but it was difficult to see anything because of the glare from the stadium lights. Had she heard right?

"*Squee!*"

"Lightning!" exclaimed Beth. The falcon dropped out of the sky like a stone, landing hard on her shoulder.

"Ouch!" cried Beth as the bird's talons dug into her skin. "What's your hurry?"

When she spotted the message bound to Lightning's leg she unwrapped it with shaking hands.

It was Flynn's handwriting, and had obviously been hurriedly scrawled.

*Door jammed. Security code 89302. Hurry!*

Beth dropped to the ground and ripped off her backpack. In a panic she fumbled with the buckle, then simply tore it off, powered by the adrenaline rushing through her body. She pulled out her laptop and powered it up. She didn't care if anybody saw the light from the screen now.

It took just an instant to log into the Dragon World system. She knew immediately what to do – the code would bypass any voice recognition system. Once in, she navigated to the cage room, and then to the garage door. A box popped up: *Malfunction. Enter security code.*

With trembling fingers, Beth tapped in the code as quickly as she could and pressed 'enter'.

# CHAPTER 40

The boys couldn't hold on any longer. Seventy-six dragons lunged at them, all desperately trying to escape. Their eyes wild with terror, they thrashed at the water, turning it to foam. Paddy saw some of them being pulled under, and re-emerging in an even bigger panic. Bravely Elton, Iris, and Big Red fought them back, but they were also fighting against their own instinct to escape.

"We have to let them out," cried Briar from behind him.

Paddy agreed. He looked across at his brother. Flynn was urging Big Red to keep the dragons back.

"Flynn, it's over! We have to let them go through the trapdoors or they'll all die!"

The look on Flynn's face was pure desperation, and Paddy felt the same. All their planning, hard work, and courage had been for nothing. The Pitbull had won.

Paddy tugged on Elton's spines to raise his head towards the opening and the safety of the arena. He dug his heels in, urging the dragon up and out of the hole.

Just as Elton's head was to about to emerge into the arena, revealing himself to the world, Paddy heard it: a screech of steel, barely audible above the deafening noise of the dragons' roars.

"Wait!" he screamed, pulling back on Elton's spines. He saw Flynn bringing Big Red to a halt with difficulty.

"What are you doing?" cried Briar, grabbing Paddy by the shoulders. "They'll all drown!" The dragons were now swimming for their lives.

Paddy felt the suction of the water around his waist first. It rapidly turned into a powerful current, and then a rushing torrent. Elton gripped the rafters against the force of it, and Paddy held onto him for all he was worth. Big Red too had been clinging to the ceiling but now suddenly dropped, and Paddy saw the huge dragon and his brother get swept away, lost from sight in the maelstrom. Iris was next, and Ahi clung to her for dear life as she disappeared. Then Elton could hold on no longer, and the last thing Paddy heard was Briar's scream of terror as they fell into the rushing water.

Paddy was under the water for what seemed like forever. Terrible noises reverberated around him, and he was struck by flailing dragons and bounced off cages. The lights of the cage room rushed by, and murky shapes appeared and receded. Then it was dark. His lungs screamed for air.

Suddenly, the current seemed to slow. Finally, thankfully, Paddy broke the surface into the cool night air, gasping desperately for breath. The torrent spread out across the concrete outside the stadium like a tidal wave, leaving behind a tangle of dragon bodies.

Paddy leaped to his feet, and immediately saw Briar close by. He grabbed her and helped her to stand, coughing and retching. He ran, with Briar close behind, both scanning the ground as they went. Paddy sprinted around and jumped over the dragons, which were picking themselves up slowly and shaking like giant dogs.

"Paddy! Briar!"

Paddy turned around. His brother was on his feet, helping Ahi up. Iris and Elton towered over them both, snickering with concern. Flynn smiled at him, eyes flashing in triumph.

"We did it," he said quietly.

The brothers came together and hugged.

"Let's get out of here," said Paddy.

But just then a voice came out of the darkness.

"You're not going anywhere," said The Pitbull.

# CHAPTER 41

The Pitbull lifted both of the tranquilliser guns, one under each arm, and aimed them at the boys. It took a supreme effort. His head swam, and his knees threatened to buckle at any moment. He was fuelled by pure rage.

When the lift to the cage room had opened, the shock of seeing it completely empty had almost done him in. He'd stood there swaying, open-mouthed with disbelief. Then he'd noticed the darkness at the end of the room. It took an age to realise that it was the steel door, or the lack of it;

it was raised, wide open! He'd set off for it, weaving from side to side, as though herding turkeys to a market. He just couldn't seem to walk in a straight line.

It was when the shattered remains of the Champagne bottle crunched under The Pitbull's shoes that he'd realised. His eyes had darted drunkenly back and forth from the rows of tranquilliser darts on the wall to the glass on the floor and the truth suddenly fell into place in his muddled mind. He remembered that the bottle had been opened, but none of his men seemed to know who'd opened it. As he lurched from side to side, struggling to stay on his feet, The Pitbull knew he'd been drugged! Those rats must have poured tranquilliser from the darts into the Champagne!

It had taken all his strength to haul himself to his feet and rip two of the tranquilliser guns from the rack on the wall. He was seeing double, and had a terrible job ramming the darts into the guns.

But now those two guns were levelled at his nemeses, the brothers. He was shocked to see his niece standing behind them, but he no longer cared about what happened to her. All he wanted was to put a dart into each of these boys.

"Stop!" the older one said, holding up his hand as though it might protect him. "It's over. The dragons have gone."

But The Pitbull could see that not all of them had taken to the sky – the green dragon, and the blue one with its baby stood behind the children. They growled like dogs. He'd shoot them next.

"Don't do this, Uncle!" cried his niece.

The Pitbull attempted to smile, but only managed a lopsided grimace. He could feel the dribble running down his chin.

"Sssay goodni..." he slurred. He was surprised to see his guns had drooped back towards the ground and with great effort he brought them back level again.

"Nooo!" screamed Briar, rushing forward.

The Pitbull squeezed the triggers, but nothing happened. The safety catches! He fumbled for them wildly, but his fingers felt like sausages. They seemed huge and numb, and seemed to move at random.

A black mist clouded his vision. Then, like a collapsing house of cards, The Pitbull crumbled to the ground in stages. First his knees went, then his hips twisted, sending him into a spiralling plummet. He was unconscious before his head hit the ground.

# CHAPTER 42

Beth walked away from the stadium, Coco trailing at her feet, Lightning perched on her shoulder. A lump stuck in her throat, a fearful dread that it hadn't worked; that not only were the dragons still imprisoned in the stadium, but now her friends were too. She feared that she was on her own, again. With Paddy, Flynn, and Briar she'd felt she belonged, for the first time in her life. She turned and searched the sky above the stadium. Nothing.

Beth resumed her lonely walk out to the highway.

Suddenly, Lightning squawked and took to the air. Then there was a buffeting sound, so faint she wondered if she was imagining it. She looked up, and thought she saw silhouettes crossing the sky. Then, unmistakably, she heard Paddy's voice! He was yelling in elation.

"Paddy!" she called. "I'm here!"

Out of the darkness swooped two colossal dragons; one green and one blue. A third, a baby, was clasped in the talons of the blue dragon. Beth was paralysed with fear, but an electric thrill of excitement travelled up her spine. They were more beautiful and fearsome than she'd ever imagined.

It took her a moment to spot the children on the creatures' backs, and she laughed with relief when Paddy's head appeared over the top of the green dragon, a broad grin on his face.

"Want a lift?" he asked.

A triumphant roar ripped through the air. Beth and the others looked up. The black silhouette of a huge dragon sliced across the face of the moon, its wings beating fast, heading due east. As they watched,

more and more followed, until the flock was so thick

it momentarily blocked out the moon.

# CHAPTER 43

When the phone rang, the Chief of Police was sitting at his desk, his head in his hands and a full glass of whiskey in front of him. He felt terrible. He'd let down his city, his country, by following The Pitbull's orders. Thankfully, his men had only managed to catch one of the children, but they told him it was The Pitbull's niece, and that she was a lovely, polite young girl. The guilt he felt was awful.

He picked up the phone. It was his head detective. "It's late, Jim," the Chief of Police said wearily.

Use the **AR Reads** app on your device to listen in to the conversation between the Chief of Police and his detective.

Simply start up the app, then point the device at this page. If you don't have a device – don't worry – just read on!

But what his detective told him made him sit bolt upright in his seat. The detective was at Dragon World. Thousands of people had called the police to complain that The Pitbull had ripped them off, and that there weren't any dragons to be seen!

"Sir, I think The Pitbull may have lost his mind," explained the detective. "It's just an empty stadium."

The Chief of Police shook his head in disbelief as the detective explained that not only were there were no dragons to be found, but that his officers had discovered The Pitbull outside the stadium, sleeping peacefully on the concrete, impossible to wake. In fact, all The Pitbull's men were asleep.
Jim suspected that they might be drugged.

The detective told the Chief that people were demanding their money back. He'd had to call in reinforcements to prevent them from rioting. He then told the Chief to turn on his television, and the Chief watched, amazed, as every news channel in the world covered the uproar created by The Pitbull's deceit.

Images flashed up on the screen of The Pitbull's early life, his success in business, the claims that he was a criminal – which no one had ever been able to prove. They showed pictures of his city tower, his house, his fleet of helicopters and his expensive cars. They briefly covered the rumours that he'd illegally bought animals from all over the world, which he kept in his own private zoo. The news story finished with an estimated calculation of how much money The Pitbull had earned from ticket sales to Dragon World. The Chief's eyes popped; it was almost twenty billion dollars.

He whistled under his breath. One thing was certain: The Pitbull was done, his reign was over. When he woke up, he'd have a mighty big headache.

The chief spoke quickly to his detective.
Here was his chance to make things better.

"Put him in handcuffs. Bring him to me," he ordered. "He's going to wake up in prison."

Just before he hung up, he had another thought.

"Wait. Also find out if there's any truth to the

rumours about this private zoo. If it's real, I want you to arrange for all the animals to be transferred to the City Zoo or released back into the wild. No one, and no creature, will ever suffer at the hands of The Pitbull again."

# CHAPTER 44

When the children arrived home, Flynn could barely stay awake. His hand throbbed with a dull ache, and he was weak with hunger and exhaustion. He knew the others felt the same.

They'd flown on the dragons' backs all the way to the coast – to Kelly's house – and then sent them off. It had been an emotional farewell, knowing that Elton, Iris, and Ahi were returning to The Island, a place of great danger. But they all knew there was no alternative; if the dragons were to remain a secret from the rest of the world they had to leave the mainland immediately. Flynn knew their dragons would lead the rest home, and he told himself that once they were there they'd stay as far from the volcano as possible.

Kelly then bundled the children into his car and drove them home. And now, as they wearily climbed the steps, the boys' parents burst through the front door, followed by sweet little Ada. Flynn and Paddy were scooped into a hug by their mother and father, and Ada clung fiercely to Briar.

"We've been watching the news," cried their mother, tears of joy streaming down her face. "We were so worried about you!"

"We'll tell you everything," said Paddy. "But first we need to introduce you to someone."

Beth stepped into the porch light.

"How do you feel about having five children?" asked Flynn.

# CHAPTER 45

The little yacht nosed its way into the calm cove just as dawn was breaking. As usual, Roger marvelled at the way his wife had been able to navigate the treacherous channel that wound its way between the sharp coral and rocks to get here.

"Nicely done, love," he called, and Millicent chuckled in reply.

He sent the anchor over the side. He could see clear to the bottom, thirty feet down, where it dug into the sand and held firm.

"Well?" said Millicent, coming to stand beside him.

Roger hadn't wanted to look at the mountain, but his wife gave him courage. Together they turned to the east. Mt Astonishing stood resplendent in the first rays of the morning sun, its snow-capped peak glowing pink.

Roger let out the breath he'd been holding. There was no smoke rising from the crater, no rocks or lava shooting into the sky. The eruption was over, and the mountain was dormant once again. He and Millicent hugged tenderly on the deck of the yacht.

Millicent smiled at him.

"Better get to work," she said.

It took all morning to ferry the timber and tools from the yacht to The Island, and all afternoon to drag it up the beach. Millicent had returned to the boat to cook their dinner, and she called out to Roger that it was ready, her voice floating across the calm bay.

"I'll be there in a minute, love," Roger shouted back. He was exhausted, but he had one thing left to do. Taking up the spade, he drove it into the ground where the first foundation of the new house would go.

If you enjoyed reading The Dragon Defenders,
I'd be so grateful if you'd take the time to rate it
or write a review on Amazon.com

Thanks,

# Get your FREE copy of
# The First Defender!

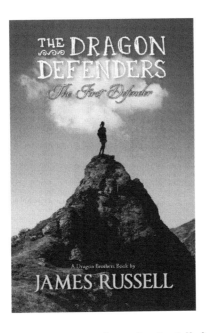

## Have you ever wondered what living on a paradise island would be like?

The First Defender – a short novel which you can download for free – includes one of the stories from the diary of Flynn and Paddy's mother. Long before they were born, when she was just a girl – and the only child on The Island – she had some pretty thrilling adventures of her own.
You might even call her the original 'Dragon Defender'.

To get your free copy, visit
**dl.bookfunnel.com/i12zk78xaa**

# About the author

Once, when James Russell was a
child, he read a book so exciting it
made his heart thump in his chest.
Now his aim in life is to write books
that will do just that for other children.
He hopes that this is one of them.

James lives in Auckland,
New Zealand with his wife and two
young sons, who love adventure in
all its forms.

# Also by James Russell

Read all the **Dragon Defenders** books!

   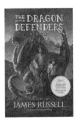 

Check out James's new series, **Children of the Rush**

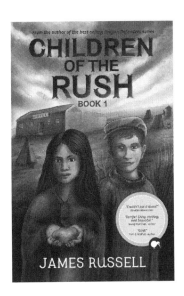

"So thrilling!"
Read New Zealand

"Captivating and fast-paced!"
NZ Booklovers

"Couldn't put it down!"
WhatBookNext.com

"Terrific! Gritty, thrilling, and beautiful!"
Weng Wai Chan, award-winning author

Available on the Amazon store or at
**www.dragonbrothersbooks.com**

Made in the USA
Middletown, DE
24 June 2023

33479623R00144